A
Bloody
Scandal

A
Bloody
Scandal

George Milner

A
Joan
Kahn
BOOK

St. Martin's Press
New York

Library of Congress Cataloging in Publication Data

Milner, George.
    A bloody scandal.

    "A Joan Kahn book."
    I. Title.
PR6063.I3796B6   1985   823'.914   85-10061
ISBN 0-312-08513-3

A Joan Kahn Book

First Edition

10 9 8 7 6 5 4 3 2 1

"I am a pretty bad fellow at bottom, and I find the pretence of virtue very irksome."

The Master of Ballantrae

"Women's faithfulness is like the Arabian phoenix. Everyone says it exists but no-one can find it."

from Lorenzo da Ponte

A
Bloody
Scandal

Farquarson was a bad lot. Deeply evil, in fact. He had risen to high rank in the Royal Navy through ambition, self-control, and courage. The first and last of these came to him easily, self-control was a less secure area.

During an adventure in the west of Ireland when he was a mere commander, accusations had been laid against him as follows: "wenching, adultery, assault, poaching, theft, shipwreck, scandal, and riot."

Guilty as charged. But these peccadilloes were both the mask and the means to encompass a crime that was truly horrific.

Since this escapade had been conducted in secrecy under a pseudonym, Their Lordships of the Admiralty had never discovered anything about it. Rumors of other scandals, mostly sexual, had reached them, not to mention improprieties. But these came under the heading of "being a bit of a lad," something the Navy inclined to admire. So the fellow had some spirit? Nelson hadn't exactly been free from sexual scandal, had he?

So long as Farquarson carried out his duties with precision and panache, Their Lordships could tolerate his womanizing, his irascible contempt, his minatory leadership, and his capricious buffoonery. There was something to be said for a chap who apparently didn't give a damn about anyone or anything except his duty.

It will be apparent that by the time he became a rear admiral, Their Lordships had not plumbed the depths of

1

Farquarson's character—in fact, far from it, the length of plumb line required was well beyond anything they could have imagined. It made perfect sense to them to appoint him Commander in Chief of the naval force sent to defend British oil rigs drilling in the South China Sea off Hong Kong. Sundry yellow persons with naval gunfire at their disposal had been making threatening noises about these rigs, the final stage of a political row about oil money: war as an extension of diplomacy by other means.

Everyone had described the Falklands war as the "last colonial war." As usual, everyone had been wrong. The Falklands had been a serious matter, a stunning feat of arms, a triumph of political will and military judgment, a show of iron nerves and sheer guts, a display—salutary to just about everybody in the world—of skill, patriotism, and justice done. But it hadn't been the last colonial war. That one was Farquarson's.

It had been widely assumed that if you were rash enough to send a modest fleet more than halfway around the world in the hope of frightening some yellow men, you would come to grief, like the Czar or Admiral Phillips. But due to luck and Farquarson's recklessness, a kind of mad victory had been achieved. At any rate, the oil rigs were still there. A few men and a few ships were at the bottom of the sea, but that was what happened in a war. Unlike the Falklands, this hadn't been a "media" war. The Navy didn't like the media men, and when Farquarson refused to take any with him he easily obtained the Admiralty's support. So that was that. It also helped Farquarson to claim a great victory from what had really been a gunboat skirmish. When he got home his officers and men weren't likely to hurry ashore to point out that less had been achieved than had been claimed. Farquarson had made them all heroes.

It was appropriate that his flagship should bear the name H.M.S. *Invisible*. The whole little war had been rather invisible, and in any case Farquarson's exploits,

2

naval, criminal, or sexual, constantly bore an air of unreality.

At the beginning Farquarson had made a frightful fuss about these absurd names, which didn't please him. What was wrong, he asked, with *Victory* or *Temeraire?* But since Their Lordships did not choose, in the run-up to a naval engagement, to change the names of their principal fighting vessels, with all the loss of confidence and administrative confusion that would result, Farquarson was stuck with them: *Invisible, Intangible, Improbable*—and all the rest.

After the event, Farquarson's barrage of propaganda—unchecked by the presence of independent observers of any kind—had set the stage for some quite different activities of a private nature. Having established himself as the conquering hero, he was now at last in a position to set in motion the murderous plot he had been hatching for some time.

It was an imposing act of effrontery and fraud to make the South China Sea skirmish sound like San Carlos Water, let alone Trafalgar.

But now the stage was set for this monster to lay the most gigantic egg.

Land of ho-ope and glory
Mother o-of the free . . .

In late August, H.M.S. *Invisible* sailed into Southampton roads, fresh from Farquarson's exaggerated victory. He had made quite certain that his flagship (plus himself) should arrive first. The objective was the glorification of Farquarson—and this not for glorification alone, more as a key to the master plan he had in his mind, his Grand Design. H.M.S. *Intangible* and H.M.S. *Improbable* could easily have arrived at the same time, but Farquarson made sure they didn't.

Despite the event and the weather, it was not like the Falklands return to the homeland. This was a local, a naval, a Portsmouth/Southampton occasion. There were no intruders from Hereford or Aldershot, SAS or Paras. The homecoming was smaller, more intense, more part of the local family. It was no less excited or patriotic for that. Such news as had arrived, filtered and doctored by Farquarson, was constructed on a slender base of truth. There *had* been a naval skirmish, ships were sunk, men were dead, Farquarson had won. So there were local crowds, plus ten thousand tourists, plus thousands more assorted nomadic patriots, all waiting to shout and cheer and sing as the great ship moved slowly toward its berth.

Rear Admiral Peter Farquarson looked down from the bridge of the flagship as the hawsers winched her bows the last few feet to bring her alongside. The mist of an August morning had cleared into brilliant sunshine. Around her an escort of a thousand small boats flew their flags and blew their hooters.

The jetty was crowded solid with people, jam-packed in their colorful summer gear, flags waving, individual banners marked to welcome Syd or Brian or Tom. Fire-fighting tugs pumped great jets into the morning sunlight, a firework display in water that dropped away into fleeting rainbows. There were two marine bands on the jetty, taking it in turn to beat the drum. The band played, the crowds sang "Land of Hope and Glory," the sailors lining the side of *Invisible* shouted back and sang with them, great bundles of thousands of balloons in red, white, and blue were released to drift away above the smoke and noise and uproar into the summer sky.

4

Farquarson viewed all this with some amusement. Soon the majority of the crew would be going ashore as heroes. They weren't *his* responsibility, of course, that was the captain's problem; Farquarson was simply flying the flag of Commander in Chief aboard the ship. He himself had been ordered two weeks earlier to leave the ship and fly back to London for debriefing and all the information that politicians, admirals, the Ministry of Defense, and all the rest now so urgently needed. Following Nelson's excellent example, he had refused. At least, he thought, Nelson had done it for a woman, something he was in dire need of. He had fended off the barrage of angry signals from the highest in the land about his disobedience with the pretext that he would return in the ship that had flown his flag with the men who had won his battle. His real reason was that he knew that his career was finished, his ambitions blighted. If there was one thing that would never be tolerated among the Whitehall Warriors, it was a successful fighting admiral. Even in a real war like World War II they had been hard-pressed to stomach men like Vian or Simpson. He'd get a knighthood—they wouldn't be able to avoid that—maybe a gong or two. Then a long silence— some obscure job—then early retirement, a forgotten man: "Pity about old Farquarson, never really made it after that spot of bother off China." Professionally he was doomed. But knowing all this, he didn't mind as much as he should have done. He had other plans, plans to retire in a manner suited to his style, if not to his prospective means, which threatened to consist merely of the pension of an admiral retired early. In fact, he was quite pleased with himself. In the event he had preempted the Admiralty, his glorious swan song—now being freely compared with the great naval battles of history—had delivered into his hands precisely the weapon that would make Their Lordships' subsequent efforts to humiliate and forget him somewhat supererogatory.

Sailors were going ashore down the gangways now, the crescendo of noise and excitement mounted. There was much fornication in prospect that night, if not earlier. Sailors and wives, sailors and girlfriends, sailors and other sailors' wives, it was going to be a night to remember. Well, good luck to them. But what about him? Was his need any less than theirs? It was not, though doubtless the young sailors would not have believed this truth about their awesome and ancient Commander in Chief, just over fifty-two years old.

Farquarson kept one woman in London, and about a third of another one. The one he kept was wholly owned and was expected, therefore, to be at his disposal. Gwenda Stubbins was just a little trollop, but her availability helped to keep him out of brothels and away from too many dangerous liaisons. The other woman was a more serious matter in every way, and the reason he contributed only about a third of her expenses was that she had a lot of money of her own.

He'd supported Gwenda for a year or two. Obviously Rear Admiral Farquarson, RN, could not be seen to be maintaining or mating with someone called Gwenda Stubbins. So the code name for Gwenda was Carruthers. Farquarson's theory was that for some mysterious reason the name Carruthers always signified a man—the last soldier of the White Raj, the head of the secret services, the British consul in Ruritania. Whoever heard of Miss or Mrs. Carruthers? Thinking of his loins, he said, "Where's Flags? Is my signals chap still around?"

"Here, sir." A lieutenant commander turned away from the group of officers who were lining the side of the bridge, watching the riotous assembly on the jetty far below them.

"I want to send a personal signal to London, please. How can we do that, now they've done away with inland cables?"

6

"Easy, sir."

"Right, then. To Carruthers, 12 Flood Row, W.8. See you nineteen hundred hours tomorrow sixteenth. Regards Peter."

"Aye, aye, sir."

Even Gwenda should be able to understand that. Not that the cable told the truth. Farquarson was going to London this very evening, once the uproar at Southampton had subsided. He couldn't escape interminable debriefing at the Admiralty tomorrow, he'd put it off already long enough to enrage them. Gwenda was one thing, just that, but his elder brother, the Laird of Corriehallie, was another. He was part of the Grand Design, and the urge to hasten matters as regards Colin had grown as a result of his thwarted ambitions and also of gossip that had reached him in the South China Sea.

Newspaper gossip, to be precise. Occasional old newspapers reached the fleet by air in the course of the long haul homeward, and among them Farquarson had found, not greatly to his astonishment, the following gossip item:

LAIRD IN SOHO BRAWL

The Laird of Corriehallie, impecunious Highland gambler and man about Soho, was ejected at about four yesterday morning from a strip-joint in Greek Street. What had gone on within these hallowed precincts before the Laird Colin, tired and emotional, landed on his butt in the street outside has not been revealed. The Laird, veteran of many similar peccadilloes, did not elect to call the police. Spice is given to the depraved antics of this ageing Gaelic ne'er-do-well by the fact that his younger brother, Rear-Admiral Peter Farquarson, RN, is Commander-in-Chief of the British Fleet at present engaged in a desperately hazardous battle in the South China

7

Sea. Differences, contrasts, blood feuds and suchlike are not uncommon among brotherly heirs to run-down Scottish estates, but surely the contrast here is especially piquant? While the elder tumbles and plunders in stews and brothels, the younger bears the responsibility for thousands of lives and the honour of the nation.

There hadn't been any jokes about this on board *Invisible*—at least none within the Admiral's hearing. Discipline requires that you don't make jokes about the Commander in Chief's brother. But there would be jokes at Nobb's all right, his club in St. James's Street, and at his other club, the Highlanders.

The laird had married money, Morrison money. Morrison, dead now, had had no sons; his fortune had gone in equal shares in trust to his three daughters, Harriet, Emily, and Julie. This made each of them wealthy. Colin had married Harriet for her money. Why Harriet had married Colin was a mystery. The marriage had broken, as any marriage to Colin (and maybe any marriage to Harriet) must do. Due to the trusts, no money had adhered to Colin, whose debaucheries did not appear to dwindle with his means. The Scottish estate was in ruins, of course, but what could you expect under such stewardship? It was to all these matters that Peter Farquarson proposed to devote his attention, starting with Harriet. Or starting, maybe, with Gwenda and from there proceeding, sailorlike, to Harriet.

Having said good-bye to his staff, he traveled to London by train in the late afternoon. He hadn't got a car at the moment—and had he owned one it would almost certainly have been in the wrong place. He would need one soon. There were a lot of things he would need soon. But all that could wait a short time; first things first. He asked the taxi to drop him at 20 Flood Row, a few doors away from the little basement flat where he maintained Gwenda in a style that, if not high, was certainly a good deal higher than that to which she had previously been accustomed.

Broad of brow, wide of feature, gray hair curling crisply, strong in build, fit and immensely energetic, Farquarson made a handsome figure even without his uniform. He could move his bulk almost noiselessly, and did so as he slipped down the steps to the door of the flat, which he opened very silently with his own key just exactly twenty-four hours earlier than the message would lead Gwenda to expect. He regarded this action as a routine precaution for a man in his fifties who kept a fairly passionate young bint of twenty for his own amusement and yet wasn't able, in the nature of his work, to spend very much time with her. What he wanted at the moment was Gwenda—but he also meant to make quite sure no one else was playing fast and loose with the property for which he paid the maintenance. In the event it was not his lust but his suspicions that were going to be gratified.

Gwenda was in bed all right, and on top of her bounced a pair of naked male buttocks. Farquarson roared into the room and caught the man's backside a tremendous welt with his right hand. Gwenda began to scream like a stuck pig while the man—young and weedy as it turned out—drew trembling off the bed, gathering bits of clothing round his privates.

Farquarson's voice was normally soft, gentle, and deep, but in the rages that overtook him quite frequently it assumed the brassy authority of a sergeant major.

"Out, you simpering oaf," he shouted. A brawny hand grasped the back of the young man's neck and propelled him inexorably—and still unclad—toward the outside door. Farquarson threw him onto the basement steps and said—before slamming the door, "It's a shame it's not winter—deep frozen snow. Just clear off and don't come back—next time I'll tear you in half." Not that there was going to be a next time; he was fed up with Gwenda.

She had changed gear now, from screaming to sniveling. Farquarson felt his pulses race all right, even more so than usual—that was the point about Gwenda, her fresh, plump, magnetic young body. But he wasn't going to have it, his fury easily supplanted his lust.

"Oh Peter, I'm so sorry—"

"It's a bit late for that. You have the damned . . . the damned . . ."

Words failed him. He grabbed her shoulder and pulled her over to lie on her front, backside up. On this he delivered three hearty slaps accompanied by an angry litany: "There goes your flat, there goes your security, there goes your allowance." He was in a fine rage.

By the end of this he was beginning to feel better, beginning to cool off a bit. Gwenda was blubbering away but more, he thought, from the future damage to her bank account than the present damage to her body.

"I'm going in a moment. Before I go I'll just ring up a few friends in New Zealand—that should cheer up your next telephone bill."

"Oh Peter, I—"

"Oh, belt up, you stupid girl. It's a damned shame, too, with a body like yours."

"I'll do anything—"

"Not with me."

He picked up the telephone and dialed Harriet's number, she who had been his sister-in-law until her marriage with Colin had ended in divorce. Harriet was tough and rich and attractive, and might come in useful in several ways at the moment.

"Harriet? It's me, Peter."

"The Conquering Hero himself." Her voice was soft and deep, what is sometimes called a bedroom voice. "Is there any chance of seeing you?"

"There certainly is," he said. "In fact, I can scarcely wait."

"It sounds rather . . . urgent," said Harriet, the words chosen carefully but the tone neutral.

"That's the idea," said Farquarson. "You were always perceptive."

"I never perceived much with that miserable brother of yours. But I might do a bit more perceiving with you." She had accepted the situation with amazing speed. "I should think this night—this very night—you could have any woman you wanted in England. So I'm greatly honored if you pick on an old hag of forty-five."

"Marvelous," said Farquarson. "We'll talk about it later. We'll get some food somewhere—Wilton's, Boulestin's, a snack at Annabel's, anything you like."

"What's happened to that teenage delinquent you keep somewhere in Chelsea? Can't you get started with her?"

"She fell down the stairs and bruised her backside."

"Oh, yes? Well, you can tell me about it later."

"I'll come round straight away. You've lots of booze, I hope."

"Lots of everything."

"See you." He rang off.

"Well, that's it," he said to Gwenda. "We shan't meet again. If you ever find another billet as good as the one you've just fouled up, send me a postcard."

He threw his key of the flat down on the floor, took a last angry look at Gwenda, marched out, and slammed the door behind him.

They ate well at Boulestin's, amid the soft lights and stylized cows, Wilton's having been thought not sexy enough and Annabel's too noisy. This meal, after all, was understood by both Farquarson and Harriet to be a leisurely and agreeable preamble to the less leisurely but even more agreeable activities planned for later. Harriet was a handsome woman who had retained her tall, full figure with no signs of middle-aged spread or sag. Her hair, worn like a neat helmet, looked sleek and black as it had always done, the color seemed natural. Her face was full and pale against the black hair and the black dress she wore, a deliberate effect. As well as being the eldest, she was the toughest of the three sisters, in Farquarson's opinion—but then they were quite a tough bunch. What would you expect from the descendants of old Morrison, a crook car-auction millionaire, a bona fide thug? Why she had married the Laird was a complete mystery to him.

Over the brandy they chatted about the South China War.

"It was quite enjoyable," said Farquarson.

"Quite enjoyable," said Harriet slowly, in that so seductive voice. "A triumph of naval arms, the culmination of a great career?"

"I was trained for it, after all. I suppose it was dangerous, but officers are trained not to notice danger, people don't always understand that. Then I was on a loser really.

If I came to grief—too bad. If I lost the war—no promotion. If I won the war—even less chance of promotion. So it was all rather boring. The fun part was making it sound like Trafalgar. I knew that would enrage Their Lordships, but then, you see, it didn't *matter* anymore, they were going to finish me off anyway. My career couldn't possibly survive a *victory*."

"It sounds like nonsense to me."

"That's because you don't understand Navy politics, the Whitehall Warriors. Anyway, it's time for a change—a new challenge, as they say. That usually means there's some disaster in the offing, but I don't have disasters."

"Now you really *do* sound like Napoleon."

"Anyway, the position is that I'm bored with them and they're bored with me."

"You have a very low threshold of boredom—is that right, Peter?"

"That's right. I like things to happen. Tell me, why on earth did you marry the Laird?"

"It was fifteen years ago, you know. We've been divorced a year now, but things still aren't sorted out. I've got a lot of my own furniture still at Corriehallie. Those fourteen years seemed like about a thousand."

"You didn't answer, did you? Why did you do it? It seems a barmy thing to do."

"Really, Peter, I've forgotten by now. It may have been partly because Emily, who's younger than me, had married and got pregnant. I was thirty then—a dangerous age for women—and I suppose I thought the world was passing me by, or some such youthful nonsense."

"Not so youthful," said Farquarson with a disarming grin. "But still—why the Laird?"

"He had a bit of tattered Celtic glamour about him . . . before he finally went to seed. It's hard to explain. There was a whiff of decayed chieftainship about him—not that Colin could ever be chief of anything except maybe the anteroom to a strip joint. We all do silly things. And then Emily's marriage fell apart too, so even the original goad turned out to have been a sham. Still, she does have Victoria."

"How old is Victoria now?"

"Eighteen."

"And Emily lives in that nice house near Hastings?"

"Yes."

"And Julie?"

"My youngest sister is something of a mystery."

"Good for her." Farquarson drank deeply from his brandy glass. His face was very close to Harriet's, his brown eyes looking straight into hers. He said, "I never liked the Laird, not from childhood. Though it was exciting to be brought up as a boy in the Highlands. We were both pretty wild, in our different ways. And it's turned out differently."

"It certainly has." Harriet laughed, a laugh that switched Farquarson on even further.

"We're not all that different really, you know. It's just that I've learned some self-discipline and he hasn't. . . . Well, discipline. Anyway, let's get the bill."

"It will be gigantic, Peter. Let me pay it as a tribute to the victorious warrior, home from battle."

Farquarson laughed. "It's handsome of you, but I'll pay it. I have other tribute in mind."

It was after midnight and they had passed the last two hours in Harriet's double bed in her palatial flat in Mayfair. They were quiet at last, drinking brandy again and smoking cigarettes. Farquarson said, "I think I'd rather like to be the Laird of Corriehallie. I was brought up there, after all. It belonged to my father."

Harriet said sleepily, "I thought you didn't like the house."

"It's a dump, but one could build a decent one there. It's a wonderful place."

"But *Colin* is Laird of Corriehallie. What are you going to do about that?"

"Colin lives dangerously, don't you think? He could get anything from cirrhosis to pox to athlete's neck at any moment. Any of them could be fatal."

Harriet pulled herself up on the pillows a little, her splendid breasts moving in the process. She was less sleepy now.

"You might have to wait a long time before your dreams came true."

"Perhaps I can speed things up a bit."

"You *do* mean something, don't you?" Harriet looked at him very closely. "There's some truth in all this. You wouldn't mind killing your brother at all?"

"Not at all," said Farquarson.

"And having murdered your brother, what would you do for money?"

"Lots of things. Marry you, for instance. We might have some fun."

"In *that* place? At *Corriehallie?* Your idea of fun is different from mine."

"Oh, I don't know," he said cheerfully. "The last hour or so I thought our ideas were rather similar."

"You fool, Peter—that was just a bit of bed. Okay, you're good at it, better than your brother, which wouldn't, let me say, be too difficult. Murder away if you want to, but leave me out of it."

"Just think it over. We could both have a very jolly time. You wouldn't have to *live* much at Corriehallie."

"So I would just trust you to be faithful among the

15

Highland wenches while you spent my money? Is that it? The Laird had the same idea."

"He spent it on stews and roulette. I'd spend it on the estate."

"From my point of view, there's not much difference, is there? Anyway, the main capital's in trust."

"You can spend trust capital on estates. You can't spend it on horses or brothels."

"Worse and worse. I end up with nothing but moorland bog."

"That's not the way I see it. By the way, have you still got that car?"

"Yes."

"The special version Jaguar, the XJS?"

"Yes."

"Could I borrow it for a few days?"

"More tribute? Why not? Of course you can. I'll give you the keys in the morning. You're staying the night, I take it."

"Yes, please. I don't want to waste the night sleeping."

"That's good."

"So nothing would get you back to Corriehallie? Not even me?"

"Only my dead body will cross the threshold of *that* place again."

"We'll see about that," said Farquarson, and began some new sexual overtures.

The next day, Monday, was the first debriefing day. To Farquarson this was a tedious and unpleasant chore. But before making his way to the Admiralty he had time to make a telephone call from the Highlanders, one of his clubs.

He had discovered from Colin's lawyer that his brother was presently holed out somewhere in Frith Street that sounded less than salubrious. The telephone was answered and he recognized his brother's whiskey tones.

"I didn't believe one word about your exploits off Hong Kong. More bullshit, I thought. Trust old Peter to get some more promotion by telling fibs."

"Look, Colin, I didn't ring you for your naval expertise."

"Why ring at all? You usually leave me in peace for years at a time."

"If you consider your life-style is peaceful, what would it take to excite you?" asked Peter Farquarson nastily. "Judging by accounts in the popular prints, your life is eventful, if not much else."

"Spare me your expertise on my private life. What do you want? You must want something."

"There are lots of things I want—not your business. But seeing the company you keep, I thought you might be able to help me."

"So what *do* you want?"

"Colin." Pause. "I want a hard man. Really hard. I don't want any old bouncer, I want a real thug. Someone young and competent, not the standard sozzled wide-boy or bruiser. Young SAS gone wrong—that's the sort of thing I want."

"What on earth do you want a chap like that for?"

"Look—do I criticize your life-style? Ask you your business? I do not. I could but I don't. You make your life, I make mine. Right? But I reckon you might know where to find the man I want."

"Are you paying for this?"

"I'll pay the chap all right, if you can find the right one."

"Are you paying me?"

"If you like," said Peter Farquarson.

"How much?"

"A fiver? What would you say?"

"I'd say five hundred."

"Okay, if he's the right man." In Peter Farquarson's plans it didn't really matter how much money he promised his brother for this particular service.

"I know one chap . . . but you'll have to watch out. Not that *I* care what he does to you."

"That's my problem, not yours. Name and address, please."

"This chap *is* ex-SAS. Killed someone for fun—got slung out. Now he hangs around Soho, touting for business. Very expensive, I'm told. But he's a rough boy, not one of your nice young sailors. Not exactly an officer or gentleman either."

"You don't know whether my young sailors are nice or not. Some of them aren't specially nice. What's your chap's line?"

"Sex and violence. Now I come to think of it, the two of you might get on rather well. If you don't . . . well, it's not likely to be a very long-lasting relationship. Nothing seems to last long with Jonathan anyway. People don't last long there either, so perhaps he's just your ticket. Perhaps I won't charge an introduction fee after all—I might just do it for fun."

"There's no need to be solicitous about my cash or my health. Just tell me where to find him. Jonathan what?"

"Silver." Colin gave a Soho address. "Now, where's my five hundred?"

"You get that later, after your thug's shown his paces."

"You might be dead before then."

"So might you. But you know me, Colin—always pay my debts. A matter of honor."

"Honor," said Colin throatily. "Honor, indeed. If you

18

mix with cannibals you may get boiled in oil, that's all. Not that *I* mind, I'd quite enjoy the smell. But how will I get the five hundred if Silver kills you?"

"You'll just have to hope, won't you? Pray for me night and day? You might be setting me up, though I can't see the point. I can see the point in *me* setting *you* up, but not the other way round. Anyway, thanks, Colin. Nice to have a chat. Provided nothing goes wrong, I'll send the cash along within a month."

"And if something *does* go wrong, as you so elegantly put it? Such as Silver deciding he doesn't like you?"

Farquarson hung up. He was bored with the conversation, and he'd got what he wanted. And the irony of the situation appealed to him. Surely this was one of the neatest bits of joinery in the Grand Design—always supposing, of course, that Silver lived up to the admirable references Colin had given him.

The debriefing began with Their Lordships of the Admiralty, in full fig and in full session. The first item was the expected row about Farquarson's disobedience in not flying home when ordered to do so. Then the inevitable questions, hours and hours of them.

"At ten hundred hours on twentieth May, why was *Invisible* zigzagging when it was known that no enemy submarines were at sea?"

"Ask the Captain."

"But you were in charge of the entire force."

"It was the Captain's decision whether *Invisible* zigzagged. He had as much information as I had."

And so on and on, Farquarson's answers becoming

ever shorter and less respectful. For years his ambitions had demanded respect amounting to what looked to him like servility. The need for that was over now. What had looked like servility to Farquarson had never looked that way to the Admiralty; they saw their past tolerance of Farquarson's outrageous behavior and recklessness as patience, a virtue in themselves that was justified because Farquarson was "a bit of a lad." The present confrontation was likely to promote second thoughts in the Admiralty, if not in Farquarson.

At a question that could (just) be construed as implying that he had at one moment positioned his flagship in a manner calculated to ensure his personal safety, Farquarson lost his temper.

"Look, I won the battle, right? I took the fleet out, I won, I brought most of it back. What more do you want?"

He stalked out of the room in a high rage.

Then he made toward Soho to find Silver.

Silver's London pad was a basement flat in Soho. Since his Chelsea love nest had gone bang, Farquarson had been staying at one of his clubs, the Highlanders in Pall Mall, and he had to make a detour between the Admiralty and Soho to change into a gray lounge suit. Now he strode through the sights of Soho, which were beginning, despite the evening sunlight, to steam up for the usual lurid business of the night. He found the number, walked down the shabby steps, and soon found himself in a gloomy, largish room with a little man who was stark naked.

Farquarson looked him over—very compact body, very trim, muscular, very fit. A perfect little fellow, about twenty-five. Did he have the brains to match? He'd got a fair idea of Silver's character from Colin.

"You're Silver?" asked Farquarson, in his deceptively quiet voice.

"But who are you? That's more to the point."

"You were recommended to me. Well, you could put it that way. It's lucky I'm not a homosexual."

"Anything you like, boss." Jonathan Silver's voice was a clipped baritone with a hint of a northern accent that Farquarson couldn't identify.

"Well, that's not what I like. Get some clothes on, for God's sake; we've got things to talk about."

"Who are you, that's the point?" Silver stared at Farquarson. The unusual combination of brilliant-blue eyes set in a saturnine complexion beneath very dark hair cut very short was disconcerting. Then the eyes widened, recognition dawned.

"If it isn't the bloody Admiral, the Conquering Hero, Lord of the Seven Seas. Well, blow me." Silver's dark little monkey face cracked in a lopsided grin.

"Get dressed, man. Then we can talk."

While Silver went to put on what eventually turned out to be a yellow kimono thing, such as is associated with wrestling, judo, and kung fu, Farquarson took stock of the flat. This one big room had a low ceiling and not much furniture. A big round table in the center used a lot of the available space, though there seemed to be only two chairs. Huge photographic blowups displaying pornographic acts were pinned to most of the wall space. A small arsenal was strewn about the floor in one corner, indicating either that Silver was very untidy or that there was nowhere else to put it. The Admiral noticed there were several guns among the junk left so carelessly about.

Silver looked even tougher in his yellow silk.

"Drink, boss?"

"What have you got?"

21

"Arrack, Pernod, poteen. Anything you like."

"Look—don't play games with me. Just find some of that Black Label you've got somewhere. Let's not waste time joking about rotgut."

Silver got out the Black Label, poured two stiff ones. They sat on the two chairs, drinks on the table.

"So what do you want?" said Silver. "When people come to me it's usually sex or murder."

"What's the going rate?"

"That depends whether it's sex or murder."

"Look—you know it's not sex, right?"

"So you want me to kill someone?"

"More than one," said Farquarson cheerfully. "What does it cost?"

"It's expensive."

"Surprise me. How much?"

"Ten thousand pounds a go, bottom rate. If it's distant or difficult, it's more."

"These are bottom rate, all right. It's still exorbitant. What about some sort of discount? I'm buying in bulk, after all."

"Look, boss, those are my rates. More than one doesn't make it easier for me. They could be *linked* without my knowing, and that's dangerous as hell."

Farquarson said, "We're going to need one of these time-and-tilt things. Bombs for cars. The 'time' bit will stop it going off too soon and the 'tilt' bit should stop it going off too late. We want an artistic result."

"Art, is it?" said Silver, pulling a face. "I wouldn't have thought art was your line."

"I wouldn't have thought crochet or petit point needlework was *your* line. But you see, people can be wrong."

"Are you joking?" Farquarson had got Silver bothered, the way he got most people bothered.

"If life is brief, *arse* is *longa,* as they say."

"But life isn't going to be brief unless I can find one of

22

those gadgets, is it? And even then you can't be sure *whose* life will be brief. Those things are sodding tricky."

"Just be careful," said Farquarson. "But the point is, can you get one?"

Silver thought and gulped his drink. Then he said, "I *could*. But won't there be a few questions when it goes off? I mean, people will ask where it came from."

"You'll just have to steal it without anyone knowing."

Silver frowned and concentrated, looking at his glass.

Farquarson said, "Aren't you making rather heavy weather of this? Anyone would think it was the Charge of the Light Brigade. It's only a couple of women and a depraved geriatric. We might even get two for the price of one, if we plan it right."

"It's full price or nothing, that's certain. Especially with one of those gadgets. Sodding unreliable, those things are."

Eventually terms were agreed—or rather, Farquarson gave in to Silver's demands. The fact was that Silver was irreplaceable, at any rate for the time being. Also, Farquarson could see that he might even enjoy Silver's company for a very short time—Silver was such a frightful little fellow.

"Could you get the gadget tomorrow?"

"Just about." Silver thought again. "It's years since they sacked me, a little break-in in Hereford isn't going to look much like me, is it? It'll give them a fit, they'll think some Irish scum have got into HQ. Still, I never did worry much about that sort of thing."

"Not a great worrier, are you?"

"I don't give a shit. But *you* worry me a little, that's my problem. I've known admirals, arrogant sods, what do you expect? But they don't employ me to kill people. Then what's all this business about *arse longas*—it just makes me wonder. I don't know whether you're a nutter, and *that's* what worries me."

23

"What worries *me* is that you might have a tape recorder in here. Shall we have a look round?"

"Now look, boss, would I have that sort of thing? Would I want my voice—the deals I do—on tape? It's a silly question. The problem is *you*. It's not the sort of thing admirals do. So what goes on? That's my worry. And have you got the money? That's my other worry."

Farquarson laughed. "Honor, that's the thing. When were you last cheated by an admiral? I'm just looking for a comfortable retirement, it's as simple as that. So we'll go to Scotland tomorrow night, then, gadget and all."

"Why Scotland?"

"We'll do a little fishing and shooting. Light a fire. Stir things up a bit."

"I hate fishing, boss."

"This will be exciting. It's not like newts and sticklebacks. What time will you be back from Hereford?"

"Before dark, the way I see it."

"Right, then. Outside Green Park Tube Station at *exactly* 0100 hours. Blue Jaguar XJS. I'll stop on the south side near the Ritz, going west. Bring the gadget and one or two guns and grenades. You'll be living rough for two or three days."

"And *you* bring ten thousand pounds. Or we shan't be going to Scotland, we shan't even get as far as Hyde Park Corner."

On this note of menace Farquarson made his departure. His next stop was to be Nobb's Club, where he was overdue to put in an appearance.

"Hello, Peter," said a rich voice. "Been potting wogs?"

There were men of all ages gathered along the semicircular sweep of the bar. Farquarson knew most of them.

"The wogs nearly potted us."

"Nice cruise, Peter?"

"It was a damned boring cruise. No women."

"Why didn't you get back sooner? We thought they'd fly you back for debriefing, and all that rot."

"They wanted me sooner. But I didn't agree."

"Like Nelson at Palermo?"

"Not at all like Nelson, or Palermo, for that matter. Nelson had a woman."

Here every man was an island.

This was the style of dialogue Farquarson enjoyed at Nobb's, one reason why he had joined the club. The members were for the most part landed, rich, boozy, caring little for tomorrow, not much either for danger or death. They enjoyed cards, backgammon, gambling, loud jokes. Aboard the great caravan to the grave they were goodish companions in Farquarson's terms—cheerfully aloof, that is, careless jesters. There wasn't much hypocrisy or pretense among them, they didn't need—and didn't intend— to bother. Make the best of a bad joke, that seemed to be their philosophy of life. Old Martin died yesterday? Shame, a good bridge player. Still, better him than me. Among them were cleverer men—also a few dangerous sharks— but to Farquarson's mind these added a bit of spice provided you didn't let them get too close. Otherwise, what did it matter, what did *anything* matter? So pass the cards, let's play.

"Can't think how you won with that bunch. Chaps like young Sandy West here."

Farquarson knew West quite well, a young naval gunnery officer, tall and strong. He didn't like West and West didn't like him. Farquarson said, "Nor me. No brains, no discipline. You never saw such a crew, Long John Silver wouldn't have had them as a press-gang."

"I'm glad I wasn't a signals man," said West.

"How come?" someone asked.

West said, in a cold and unfriendly voice, "At least I was able to shoot off shells—not just a great long line of bullshit."

Before this could go any further, Lord (Bertie) Varndale, who had been chatting with a young stockbroker called Jenner, broke in: "I see old Colin's been making a fool of himself in Greek Street again."

"Yes. He's got a sore arse, apparently. There seems to be a lot of that around lately."

"He's lucky if that's all he's got," said Varndale. "What happens to the family estates while the Laird explores the sex life of Soho?"

"They fell to pieces ages ago."

"I suppose it's just as well he's not a member here."

"It is," said Farquarson, a touch of dark anger in his voice.

"I don't know about that," said Jenner. "I know some people who might find his advice quite useful."

"And what does *that* mean?"

"The trouble is"—again Varndale broke in deliberately, to maintain the peace—"that you can't get rid of a club member, however much of a shit he is, unless he goes to prison or becomes bankrupt. There just isn't any way of doing it. That's why they make such a fuss about the elections, but mistakes still happen. A chap I knew, rather an old grandee, once said you should get your son into all the best clubs when he's young, before everyone finds out what a shit he really is. A good point, since you can never get them out."

"Why don't we play bridge?" said Farquarson. "I saw Trevor Spengler in the card room, all on his own. Waiting for someone to turn up, presumably."

So when they'd collected drinks Varndale, Jenner, and Farquarson moved off to join Spengler in the card room. Spengler was of special interest to Farquarson, since he was a Morrison trustee, responsible for the capital and income held on behalf of Harriet, Emily, and Julie.

Spengler was about fifty-five, crumpled face, baldish. He was good at business, less so at bridge. He'd been a good deal younger than old Morrison when they'd both been busy making a gigantic fortune out of car auctions. Morrison had trusted Spengler. How Spengler had become a member of Nobb's was something of a mystery, but stranger things had happened.

The card room was lit only by green-shaded lights hung low over the tables on long chains from the ceiling, as in a casino. There were four tables but none was in use. Spengler sat alone at one of them. When they had cut, Farquarson ended up with Varndale as partner, Jenner opposite Spengler.

"Ten pounds a hundred?" asked Farquarson.

Spengler glanced at him, cool and amused.

"Why not?" said Varndale.

Jenner said, "What's wrong with the club stakes?" The club stakes were a pound a hundred.

"Just about everything," said Farquarson. "A waste of time."

"You'll have to find someone else, then," said Jenner. "I won't play higher than the club stakes."

"Oh, let it go, Peter," said Varndale. "Let's get on with it, for goodness' sake. We can do something different

27

later, when we're playing against each other."

So club stakes were agreed, with no good grace on the part of Farquarson. In the event there wasn't to be a "later."

The winning hand of the rubber went like this:

NORTH

(Lord Varndale)

♠ K 8 5 4
♡ J 9 3 2
♢ A K 10 8
♣ A

WEST	EAST
(Tony Jenner)	(Trevor Spengler)

♠	J	10			♠	9	7		
♡	7	6	5		♡	Q	8	4	
♢	J	3	2		♢	7	6	5	4
♣	J	9	8	5	4	♣	K	10	6	3

SOUTH

(Peter Farquarson)

♠ A Q 6 3 2
♡ A K 10
♢ Q 9
♣ Q 7 2

The bidding:

North	East	South	West
1 NT	Pass	7 NT	Pass
Pass	Double	Redouble	

Jenner (West) played a low club.

"It's not your lead," said Spengler quietly. "Take it back."

Here was a fine old muddle. In bridge the player who first calls the suit in which the hand is eventually contracted is the one who plays it. This player is called the declarer. The first lead from the defense has to come from the player on the left of declarer before the dummy hand, the hand of declarer's partner opposite him, goes down on the table. It is not unknown for wrong leads like Jenner's to be made by mistake, especially after a few drinks and a dramatic auction. It doesn't happen at the top level of bridge, but this party at Nobb's were not top-level players, as this bidding sequence clearly demonstrates. No doubt the World Bridge Federation has set out somewhere what the penalties are when such a disaster crops up in Tournament Bridge. At the club rubber level these dilemmas are usually resolved in a friendly manner under local conventions and manners: Such civilized customs didn't carry much weight when Farquarson was around, it being his usual habit to make up the rules as he went along. Hence the following weird proceedings.

"He can't take it back," said Varndale. "This is a grand slam redoubled. I don't know what the hell we do next."

"We claim the slam and the rubber," said Farquarson.

"That's a bit thick," said Jenner.

"Look, we can claim it. But seeing we're gentlemen

29

playing for low stakes I suggest, if Bertie and Trevor agree, that I play the hand and Bertie becomes dummy. Then the club lead can stand."

After some prolonged palaver this bizarre solution was agreed. Spengler demurred, but in the end there was nothing he could do about it. Anyway, at only a pound a hundred . . .

Bertie's hand went down. Farquarson took a look and claimed thirteen tricks.

"What about the queen of hearts?" said Spengler.

"The queen of hearts is in the wrong place. If your double makes any sense at all."

"The real trouble is that the *declarer*'s in the wrong place. And suppose the diamonds don't break?"

"Let's lay them all down and see."

The diamonds didn't matter, the queen of hearts *did* fall on a finesse, so Farquarson was bound to make thirteen tricks as bid.

No one was very pleased about this except Farquarson, though Spengler, the one with most to complain about, seemed to regard the whole thing as a joke. Varndale said to Jenner, "I'm sorry, Tony. That was a bit of a shambles. But you shouldn't have led."

"No," said Jenner angrily. "I shouldn't. And I shouldn't have been bullied by the Admiral into the rest of the proceedings, either. It was a bloody scandal—I'll report it to the Chairman of the Card Committee."

"Do what you like," said Farquarson. "The whole thing's ridiculous."

"It's not *just* ridiculous, it's scandalous."

"Oh, come on, Tony," said Varndale placatingly. "It's not the end of the world. Come and have a drink with me—we'll leave Peter and Trevor to talk it over."

The two men strolled away to the bar.

"It certainly was a bit hot," said Spengler, mildly amused. "I don't know that I'd have gone so quietly at ten pounds a hundred. The bid was wrong too."

"We made it," said Farquarson. "What's wrong with that?"

"It lacked . . . delicacy." Spengler's expression was amused and reflective. "It certainly didn't lack finesse, it actually depended on it. I shouldn't have doubled, though it might have worked. In fact, even six is a gamble. If the queen of hearts is wrong, you're two off with the king of clubs. As it happens, the horse-trading about who plays it doesn't make any difference. It was silly of Jenner, though . . . a most amazing transaction altogether."

Evidently Spengler had decided to regard the episode as a joke.

"Well, you owe me twenty-nine pounds."

Spengler counted out the money. He said, "I can see why Jenner's upset. Made a fool of himself, got shoved around, lost a big hand and some money. Strictly speaking, I should have to say that you and Bertie behaved rather well. The committee's bound to ask me if he really does complain."

Farquarson put the money in his wallet.

"I don't give a damn about the committee. Tell me, Trevor, you know about my brother. How do these Morrison trusts work? You're a trustee, aren't you?"

Spengler drew a leather cigar case from his pocket. He offered one to Farquarson, who refused. Spengler lit up in a leisurely way and leaned back in his chair, inhaling contentedly.

"That's not your business, Peter, is it?"

"No. But none of these trusts are really secret— they're recorded in places like the Capital Taxes Office. I could probably get one out of Colin if I ever caught him sober. Don't tell me if you don't feel like it."

"Why not? You could find out, as you say. The trouble is, no one quite knows how they *do* work. Old Jimmy— Morrison, my old partner—was obsessed with progeny. Having no son, he knew his name couldn't go on, but he was dead keen that his *line* should. The trusts were loaded

toward anyone who did some breeding. The three girls—
Harriet, Emily, Julie—all had their share, safe and settled
for life, of course. Now if they died in succession, which is
the only judgment common sense can make, Emily succeeds Harriet, Julie succeeds Emily, and *if there's no progeny,* the money—of which there would be a very great deal
by then—goes to charity. If there's male progeny, *all* the
money goes to the eldest male heir. Emily married, of
course, but the marriage broke up, like Harriet's. So that
lets out Broadhill, her husband, who's in the same position
as Colin—not that either of them could ever have been
heirs. But Emily had progeny, i.e., Victoria. Now, given
the above three deaths without more and male progeny—
and they're all getting a bit old for it—what happens next?
Well, as usual, the lawyers don't know, and they can see
some fat money wrangling about it.

"So it depends on the order in which people die, who
produces progeny, above all, who produces *male* progeny.
An adventurer," Spengler went on sardonically, "who
wanted to get the maximum pile of old Morrison's fortune,
would be best advised, it seems, to proceed as follows:
Murder Harriet, murder Emily, discover whether Julie is
too old to breed and, if not, to marry her and get on with
it. If she's too old, he should try marrying Victoria. That
would be his best logical line, but even so, if neither of the
ladies produced a *son,* the charities might still win. And the
lawyers certainly would. It's not really at all a good pitch
for adventurers, it's too complicated and uncertain; much
easier to go and murder somebody else. You could rely on
old Jimmy to be pretty astute."

"I can't see anyone tackling that lot," said Farquarson.
"These family trusts are hell."

"It's amazing what you can do with them. It's all lawyers, as you know. I know a man whose eldest son got together with his mother—the son's grandmother—and they
conspired to cheat him out of all the family trusts. Suc-

ceeded too, all legal and aboveboard, and the wretched young man didn't even have a son, for goodness' sake. Amazing—not at all what the original funds were intended for. Still, it's what happened."

"Odd things happen, all right," said Farquarson. "Many thanks, Trevor, a splendid little tangle. Goodness knows what Colin does for loose cash. Let's go and look for some food. Sorry about the grand slam—it seemed fair enough to me."

"It seemed fair enough to me too. Just. It might have been different if you'd been playing ACOL."

"ACOL is for computers," said Farquarson. "No one can remember it."

"Most good players have ACOL at their fingertips," said Spengler with more spirit than usual. "Don't scorn ACOL."

"Good old ACOL," said Farquarson. "You can't lose with ACOL."

Spengler smiled his unreadable smile and they moved off toward the bar on their way to the dining room.

"Why did you authorize the aircraft strike at 1900 hours on Thursday 3rd June . . . ?"

"On the long sea voyage homewards, after you had failed to obey our instructions to return at once by air, you no doubt had time to assemble from immediate memory an exact record of . . ."

And so on, all day Tuesday, with a break for lunch that was more austere than usual. Farquarson rightly interpreted this lack of conviviality as a mark of Olympian displeasure with himself, but he didn't care anymore. His mind was on other things. After this meal, conducted largely in an arctic silence, he was able to slip away to visit his bank before the afternoon session of the conference began; more and more boring questions.

At the bank he asked for ten thousand pounds in used notes. The pretty, pert, redheaded, freckled, very young bank teller was fascinated by Farquarson, and not only by his curious cash withdrawal—she couldn't believe her luck, apparently. "An Admiral," she kept whispering as she counted the notes. *"The* Admiral. Lord of the Seven Seas." For his part, Farquarson lusted after her.

Back at the Admiralty conference his briefcase, bursting now with fifty-pound notes, lay by his feet as von Stauffenberg's had once done in Hitler's forest hut, and to Farquarson it seemed to tick even more loudly. What would Their Lordships think if the clasp broke and the dirty notes exploded all over the conference room? It wouldn't do the Grand Design much good. It was better to concentrate on the incessant questions.

At the Highlanders that morning the post had brought him a collection of begging letters and bills from Gwenda, which he had thrown in the wastepaper basket.

In the evening—when at last he got away from the Admiralty, having made it clear that he would not be coming back for a few days, whether they wanted him or not—he went to Harriet's flat. He needed her car. In it they drove to Wilton's: not so sexy tonight; Farquarson had other things on his mind, though Harriet didn't know it.

After another pleasant but expensive meal she asked, "Are you coming back to the flat tonight?"

"I wish I could." His loins did wish it. "But I have to do something about Gwenda, she of the sore backside."

"And what are you going to do about her in my car in the middle of the night?"

"For God's sake, Harriet, there *are* other things."

"Are there? Well, it needs explaining."

"Just wait and see," said Farquarson.

He dropped Harriet at her flat and parked the Jaguar near the Highlanders. From his room in the club he gathered the gear he was going to need—including a huge carton of Mars bars—and stored them in the boot of the car. Then he managed to find some backgammon going on at the Highlanders; failing that, he would have had to go to Nobb's, where there was certain to be a game at this time of night. To the amazement and incredulous bewilderment of a few fellow members, he succeeded in losing three hundred pounds in very short order. At a quarter to one in the morning he announced that he was going to bed. At 0100 Wednesday he pulled the Jaguar alongside Green Park Station, south side of Piccadilly.

Silver was there, with two rucksacks. Farquarson pressed a switch that opened the boot electrically. Silver threw in one of the rucksacks, which landed with a fearful metallic clank. The other he put on the back seat with rather more care. Silver wore a black leather jacket and tough lightweight green trousers of the drainpipe variety but without creases, almost cylindrical. Farquarson said, "I hope that lot you threw into the boot doesn't include the gadget. That's no way to treat it."

"It doesn't," said Silver, getting in. "Why's the boot full of Mars bars?"

"In case you forget your rations."

"Not likely, boss. Where's the cash?"

Farquarson handed over the money, and wasn't surprised to see it counted deftly and swiftly under the map light.

"It's three hundred pounds short," said Silver.

"A bagatelle."

"These are three hundred smackers, boss." A note of chilling ice had crept into Silver's slight twang of an accent. "Don't play the fool with me—it's dangerous."

"I expect you counted them wrong. Anyway, if we spend half the night here chatting in a car stuffed with bank notes, a cop will turn up. And where will that leave *you?* Think of your luggage."

"Or *you?*"

"Make no mistake," said Farquarson, "I can get away with just about anything at the moment. Remember that. Remember it well."

"Where's the money? That's the point. The three hundred pounds? I could clear off now with this lot—and what could you do about it?"

"I might make some suggestions about how things go missing from Hereford. You see," Farquarson went on quietly, "I can make threats too. Hide the stuff away—let's get going."

"But where's the three hundred pounds?"

"I lost it playing backgammon. I'll add it on to the next payment, when you've actually done something to earn it."

"I don't believe it. You can't be *that* bad at backgammon."

"The point was to attract attention. It all seems a lot of fuss about nothing much."

"Your idea of money is different from mine."

"And there, young man," said Farquarson, "you're absolutely right."

Silver stuffed the bundles in various pockets of his jacket. Twenty minutes later they were on the M.1.

The night was clear and warm, visibility perfect. The Jaguar flew down the fast lane, flashing the hundred-miles-an-hour sluggards out of the way. Lorries in the slow and middle lanes seemed literally to be going backward. After furious flashing by Farquarson, even Rollses and sportsters moved over to the middle lane, then fell behind like little stationary models. Even so they could talk well enough in the saloon. Silver said, "Do we have to go this pace, boss? It's like being in the SAS."

"I read somewhere that if you're going over a hundred and forty miles per hour, the police radar doesn't work. And none of those old Rovers can catch us. Even their Jaguars won't catch this one. Anyway, it saves time."

"It certainly doesn't save petrol. We must be doing about five miles per gallon."

"There's an oil glut."

"We should be able to make a nasty hole in that—as well as anything else that happens to cross our path."

"For God's sake, man, we're only driving along a road. Anyone would think we were doing stunts in a prototype autogyro. And I don't mean to be seen—I don't want us pottering round the Grampians in midmorning, or when the pubs start to open."

"How far is it then?" asked Silver.

"It was five hundred and thirty-five miles when we started. It's getting less, though."

"I can see that. So what time do we arrive?"

"We should average about a hundred and ten on the motorways, allowing for petrol stops and so on. Say we average about sixty on the other roads at this time of night. An overall average of eighty gets us there at about 0730. There shouldn't be many people about then."

"Well, I think I'll have a snooze. It's not as though the excitement's unbearable, is it? And I suppose you know what you're doing."

"No problems, unless this contraption blows up on us. That could be quite a serious bother, but I don't suppose it will. Snooze away, you'll be glad of it later."

"You don't need sleep?"

"Not much," said Farquarson.

In the event it was just after 0700 that the car slid past the empty and derelict lodge that stood where the gates had once been at the end of the Corriehallie drive. A minute or so later it vanished into a great barn some hundred yards down a rough track that led away from the barrack of a house that was Corriehallie.

There was plenty of light in the huge, ramshackle barn. It fell clear through the open door, and seeped in through a hundred cracks and holes caused by fallen tiles and splintered timbers. Some old bales of straw had disintegrated into an amorphous heap, no doubt a haunt for rats and mice. There was an ancient Land Rover, neglected and derelict in a corner.

"Good," said Farquarson. "I was counting on that thing."

"I wouldn't say it would go," said Silver. "Anyway, I'm hungry."

"Didn't you bring any rations?"

"Yes. But it's a bit early to start on them."

"There's a bagful of Mars bars in the boot. I'm going to have one for breakfast—then I'm going to sleep."

"How long are you sleeping for? What do you want me to do?"

"Wake me at eleven hundred. Meanwhile do a recce. And try to make the Land Rover work. Then we'll go fishing."

By 11:30 A.M. they were ready for the river. The Land Rover was firing on two or three cylinders, gulping and puffing. Farquarson had collected two old fiberglass salmon rods from the house. He had also assumed the most peculiar disguise, for which he had brought the wherewithal from London. A false beard was the most important ingredient, but the real moleskin trousers with apron held up by string plus a decrepit straw boater made him look like the head gardener at a run-down Victorian estate. It was not Farquarson's intention to make himself invisible or unremarkable; his intention was to make it inconceivable that he could be Admiral Peter Farquarson.

He knew every current and ripple of the river, every swirl and lie. There would be no gillies now. Amid the general decay and neglect there was a chance that no one had even taken the trouble to let the beats, a perfectly good source of income provided the banks had been kept clear, which, again, he doubted.

The road was close to the river, but left a very precipitous path to be negotiated on foot. He ran the old car into a thicket of small trees so that it could not be easily seen. Soon both men had scrambled three hundred feet down the path, which was often rough, sometimes marshy, and always overgrown. At the foot they reached the river, a rocky torrent that grew more placid where the tails of the pools spread out before narrowing again into the next stretch of rapids. The branches of silver birch and conifer overhung it sufficiently to deter any prospective angler from renting it, but not far enough to deter Farquarson.

Two salmon jumped in the middle stream, then another in the slower water below.

"They look safe enough to me," said Silver. "It's a bloody jungle."

"Just watch," said Farquarson. "The place hasn't been fished—they haven't seen a fly for months."

Farquarson was about the best fisherman around. In twenty minutes he had a salmon on the bank, though he'd drenched his moleskins landing it.

"It's all yours," he said to Silver. "I'm going back to the house. I'll be back here by 1500. You ought to have half a dozen on the bank by then."

"Like hell," said Silver. "But I can think of a way."

This was what Farquarson had reckoned on. He said, "Tight lines."

Twenty minutes later the Land Rover was back in the barn. Farquarson walked out into the sunlight to revisit the haunts of his youth.

It was with mounting anger that he surveyed the decaying barrack of a house, the potholed driveway where grass and mosses grew. Some slates had fallen off the roof, some windows were broken. He remembered it as it had been before the war, trim, occupied, busy, useful. Toward the end of the war, as he grew toward manhood, he had spent his holidays from Dartmouth at home. Then the house was under siege, the men and women it needed to run and maintain it had gone to war. But the decay was slow and controlled and his father—when not pursuing women, which had been his principal occupation—had fought to arrest it. His poor mother had struggled on in the house, which grew ever colder as fuel ran short. But for the boys, Colin and himself, it had been exciting. The very improvisation needed to keep anything going at all was fun to them, it broke the formal routines and provided a constant sense of emergency. But it had all been too much for his mother, whose strong spirit had eventually been broken by the ceaseless infidelities and the decrepit estate around her. After the war, when his father was able to recruit a tiny labor force and slowly start the process of restoration, she had died. His father's antics thereafter, for all their promiscuous eccentricity, did not include the neglect of the property. It was only after he had died and Colin had inherited an adequate little estate that the rot really set in. It was all Colin's fault, and Farquarson felt dizzy with rage just to think of it.

He walked down the drive. The shingle foundations were breaking through the potholes in many places, forming little heaps of polished, slippery stone. Great branches that had fallen off trees had been pulled roughly to one side of the track to clear a path, but nothing else had been done to keep the road open or maintain it. Soon a great tree would fall and bar it, and after that no one would do anything at all. The whole drive would subside, the bracken and mosses would seize it and tear it apart. The house would be cut off and quickly fall into final ruin. There would be nothing left of the Farquarsons of Corriehallie, or their inheritance. Everything depended on Peter Farquarson, and his Grand Design.

When Farquarson had scrambled far enough down the precipitous path to get a clear view of the river he saw salmon after salmon flying through the air. He had expected something of the sort, it was just the sight itself that was curious.

At the tail of the long pool, Silver was standing up to his waist in water, almost in midstream. Dead salmon floated toward him, past him, away downriver behind him. Silver seized every dead fish that he could reach from where he stood, grabbed it around the tail with both hands, and swung it in a high arc through the air and onto the shingle bank that formed the shoreline to the bottom of this particular pool. Already fifteen or so of the great glistening creatures lay scattered on the stones, thrown higgledy-piggledy at random. And the number kept growing as more silver giants sailed through the air to land with a smacking splat, then slither and lie still among the slippery stones. Farquarson made all speed to the bank, and once within hailing distance of Silver shouted—while dodging the missiles, "What's happened now?" He could guess, though.

"I got the better of them, boss. I fooled them." Silver began to make his way toward the shore, since the supply of dead fish borne toward him by the current was now rapidly failing.

"You tossed in a grenade?" said Farquarson.

"Right. It was so bloody boring. And I got caught up in the brambles all the time. You'd never have guessed there were so many, would you? There seemed to be only two or three in the pool—and now there must be twenty on the bank. Masses more floated past, a hundred I should think; I couldn't reach them."

"What are you going to do with the ones on the bank?"

"They're worth money," said Silver. "I'll flog them in the nearest town."

"And who's going to carry them up the cliff? They must weigh two hundred pounds or more."

"You help, and I'll let you off some of the three hundred pounds you owe me. These are quality fish, boss, worth three pounds a pound."

"If you say so," said Farquarson, who knew the August price was much lower.

Silver was quite excited.

"What a haul, boss. What a killing. Better than miserable roach in the gravel pits."

"One of them belongs to me. Well, I suppose strictly speaking, they *all* belong to me."

"I thought gentlemen's guests could keep their own catch."

"Did you?" said Farquarson. "Well, you thought wrong. But even if you'd thought right—look at it again. I'm not a gentleman, you're not a guest, and you didn't catch them. Right?"

"We'll load them into that busted old banger, then I'll drive off and flog them. You're too conspicuous—you look like a circus clown."

42

"We'd better both get started up the cliff. Tonight we have some serious business and the day after tomorrow you do some work—what you're paid for. You seem to have bagged one or two sea trout and brown trout in the holocaust—I think I'll put some in my pockets in case we get hungry."

He did so.

They carried the huge weight of fish up the precipice and stowed them in the Land Rover. Silver drove and dropped Farquarson off at the derelict lodge at the end of the drive. Then he went off to sell the fish.

Farquarson laughed to himself as he walked back up the drive. So Silver thought he would get the better of the local fish experts, did he? He was in for a painful surprise there.

For some reason Farquarson was squeamish about butchery. A few stunned salmon was one thing, but what came next was another. But it had to be done; and that meant Silver had to do it. He'd probably enjoy it anyway.

They ate grilled trout and Mars bars by a little fire inside the barn. As the light began to fail, Farquarson said, "I'm going to have a nap. You're going shooting."

"Yes?"

"You've got a small machine gun, I saw it. You drive the Land Rover up the track to the north—I'll show you—as far as you can go. Up on the tops—it's not all that high up, not like Balmoral—you'll find deer. Just let rip with the gun and slaughter as many of them as you can. Be back here by midnight."

Silver set off.

Farquarson drowsed. He wasn't going to get much

sleep tonight; this was the only chance. After a couple of hours he half-heard—through veils of sleep—distant machine-gun fire. Later he heard the old banger grunting and puffing along the track, and was wide awake when Silver came into the barn.

"I suppose you know what you're doing," said Silver. "I didn't like that much."

"You're not here for what you like. Now, let's go and burn the house down."

Farquarson lit a cigarette. In the lighter's flare he saw Jonathan Silver's bright-blue eyes, so oddly combined with his dark complexion and black hair, widen and shine in delight and anticipation. Jonathan said, "The old homestead itself? What do you want to do that for?" For all his excitement he was trying to keep cool, watching Farquarson closely.

"It's a drafty old pile. I bet it's not insured properly, either."

"Your childhood home? Your nursery years? That's hard to imagine, I must say. The very place where Our Hero grew up?"

"Oh, belt up," said Farquarson. "It's just an old dump."

"Is anyone living there?"

"I shouldn't think so. We'd have seen them by now, or signs of them. Anyway, we shall make quite a noise, carting paraffin and smashing furniture."

"What happens if the racket brings out a butler and a housemaid?"

"I don't think it will—I think it's empty. Anyway, we can hide, can't we?"

"Well, okay, whatever you say. You're the boss. After all, it's your house, more or less. It should go up with quite a whoomf."

Two hours later the bonfire was ready, a great stack of broken furniture was piled high in the center of the main hall, and drenched in paraffin. Farquarson said, "It's a

44

shame not to stay for the bonfire. But I must go. A single match should do it—then you make for the forest. Here's another trout." He pulled one out of his pocket and handed it to Silver.

"What are you going to do?"

Farquarson looked at his watch. 0300.

"Breakfast at Nobb's, with any luck," he said cheerfully. "You'll have to hide out in the woods all day today, then tonight, then all day tomorrow—that's Friday. At *exactly* 2300 hours Friday night you ring me at Nobb's—here's the number. Say you're calling from Canada, ask to speak to me urgently, make a fuss."

"What's the point of that?"

"To give you the car number and train time, of course. This chap will travel north on the Motorail on Friday night, I'm sure of it. He won't have time to get organized on Thursday, and he won't travel any other way, he never has. It'll be the night Motorail to Edinburgh on Friday night."

"Just what happens if he doesn't?"

"I'll pay you a cancellation fee—the rich man's wooden spoon. But he will, you'll see. So—right. You've got to hide out for approximately forty-three hours. Then it's 2200 hours Friday evening. Then you find a telephone and ring me at Nobb's at 2300 hours. After that you've got lots of time. You steal a car from wherever it suits you, drive down to Edinburgh with the gadget, find the Motorail unloading bay, and stick the thing under the car when no one's looking. Then you can do what you like."

"You make it sound so simple. What do I do with the stolen car?"

"Why not drive it to Stirling and catch a train down from there? That should add to the confusion. Don't drop any of those wads of notes around anywhere. Make sure you burn the Mars bars wrappings too."

"Don't forget the three hundred pounds."

"I'll give you ten thousand three hundred pounds next time. If all goes well. Less the value of the salmon.

Remember—you haven't done *anything* so far—except drive around in luxury cars, salmon fishing, deer stalking, and bonfires. You should be paying me, really."

"I didn't *get* much for the salmon. Crook Scots."

"Well, I'm off. Give me ten minutes to get these togs off and clear the Jaguar out of the drive. Then you light up. Have a jolly time. Tight lines."

"See you, boss. See you with lots more money."

On Thursday Farquarson had time on his hands, time he did not intend to devote to the Chiefs of the Defense Staff. It had turned out to be too late for breakfast when he reached Nobb's at around 1000 hours, service stopped at 0930. He'd put a Mars bar in his pocket against this eventuality, so he ordered a large Bloody Mary and made this his breakfast, along with the chocolate concoction. He slept the rest of the morning away at the Highlanders, where later he ate a substantial lunch.

He must get to the bank before it closed, his first important visit.

At the bank counter he was unlucky to have to deal with the same cashier as before, the one from whom he'd got the previous £10,000 in a brief escape from the Admiralty debriefing during the bad-tempered lunch on Tuesday. A pert little redhead—he could see a good use for her in bed, indeed he could vividly imagine it, but as his teller for a second time she was likely to be an inquisitive nuisance. But if he were to say, "Buzz off, send the busty one over," it would only cause more gossip about his curious cash withdrawals.

So he said, rather austerely, "Good afternoon. I want

to draw ten thousand pounds in notes from my deposit account, please."

"Good afternoon, Admiral. Of course. Anything you say. The other lot didn't last long, did it? It was Tuesday."

"Just get the cash," said Farquarson. "I'll give you a check."

"Aye, aye, sir. I like a man who spends money."

"I don't spend it, I burn it. It's cheaper than coal."

"Ooh, I must ask my dad about that. I don't think he'll agree, really. He thinks ten thousand pounds is a lot of money."

"Well, I don't," said Farquarson, "also, I haven't got all day to gossip about it. I want to light the fire, keep warm. So just get going."

"You are a one. My dad said you had the fleet arranged all wrong, he says if he'd been there—"

"Look, I'm sure your dad would have been better at winning the war than I was. But he hasn't got ten thousand pounds, has he? On the other hand, I *have* got it, and all that's standing between me and my money is you gossiping about your dad. What's your name?"

"Pettina."

"Come off it," said Farquarson. "Surname?"

"Camelot."

"How could a thing like that happen?" said Farquarson.

"I'll tell you. When my grandmother was in Barbados—"

"You won't tell me," said Farquarson. "Get the money."

"If you want to be shirty—"

Farquarson banged on the counter. He couldn't reach her to wring her neck, the bullet-proof glass division had been installed to foil such intentions.

"I don't want to be shirty, I just want to keep warm. Get the cash or I'll ask to see the manager."

"You're attracting a crowd. You're keeping all these people waiting."

And indeed the queue behind Farquarson was getting longer and more restless all the time, whispers of "Hurry up, mate," and so on.

"If you weren't so damned chatty I'd have my money by now."

"I'll tell them all who you are. *That* will cause quite a stir."

"If you tell them that," said Farquarson, "they'll all be swarming round taking pictures, lots of them will have pocket cameras, video gear and stuff. And *that* will mean that my bank balance appears in all their family albums and videos. So you get the sack—right?"

Pettina jounced off cheerfully to get the cash and came back with bundles of it: packages of shiny new notes.

"This is no good," said Farquarson, "get some old ones. This fancy modern rubbish doesn't burn properly."

"I got them specially for you—seeing who you are."

"Can't you remember as far back as Tuesday? Old ones, girl, the same as before. Old is best."

"You should know," said the girl.

The murmurs, whispers, and occasional shouts from the queue behind were becoming more audible, their content less and less flattering. Soon the bank would close, and if Farquarson didn't hurry up, they'd be left stranded. Luckily no one had recognized him.

When the old notes had been brought, sorted, counted, and handed over, Farquarson said, "How about dinner tonight? Savoy Bar, seven o'clock."

"Ooh, I couldn't," said Pettina.

"Right then. I'll see you in the Savoy Bar, seven o'clock. Meanwhile you'll have to do something about this mob."

And he marched out, his suit pockets bulging with bank notes.

48

Having stashed the money away at the Highlanders, his next call was to be the Central Intelligence Offices. He hadn't told them he was coming, he knew how these places worked. Announce your arrival and security would be tight, everyone on their toes and keen to show zeal. Just saunter in and you'd probably find the television scanner was busted and the guard asleep. If it had been so difficult to get his own money out of his own bank, what was it going to be like to find and steal a secret poison from the heart of the intelligence system? Probably dead easy.

And so it proved.

There was security of a sort, but once they'd checked who he was he was left to ramble around on his own. The object was to palm and pocket one of the tiny objects known as "Bulgarian pellets," the things Bulgars stuck on the ends of their umbrella spikes to kill each other with. What did they call the stuff? Ricyn? A likely story. No one could ever have believed all that nonsense about mysterious poisons, instant, untraceable—let alone the idea that the Bulgars could have invented the things. When did the Bulgars ever invent anything, let alone something as subtle as this? They were too brutish and stupid. This fancy pellet had undoubtedly been brewed in some Western laboratory, probably American or English, most probably English. Who'd let some of them get into the hands of what Bulgars for what reasons was one of those mysteries that might be solved one day by the espionage novelists but wasn't likely to be solved by anybody else.

There were more ways than one to skin a cat, of course. But for the individual he had in mind he needed something rather unexpected.

Back at Nobb's he whiled away the time till 1830 hours playing bridge. He lost thirty-three pounds.

Although he quite liked Pettina's style, he didn't anticipate that dinner at the Savoy was going to be especially scintillating. It would be a touch of the Lolitas, of course, but that wouldn't be anything new; Gwenda hadn't been the only one in the past. He didn't really want to hear how her dad would have conducted the South China war, or what it was her grandmother had done in Barbados that ended with the bizarre consequence of the family's being called Camelot and the girl herself Pettina. You'd think it would have to be something perfectly extraordinary, but no doubt in the event it would turn out pretty banal. After all, it was her body he was after, that was what he was paying the bill for.

There would probably be a row later, more letters to throw away like the ones that kept coming from Gwenda. One might even speculate that someone called Mr. Camelot might make an extra special nuisance of himself, not least since he apparently supposed that he already enjoyed the prerogatives of an admiral without having fathomed how far those prerogatives might be made to extend.

A more immediate problem was where—assuming that all went well—the evening was to be consummated. Pettina's dad, if he existed at all, would scarcely welcome such proceedings under his own domestic roof. Worse still, Farquarson might even get a lecture on the South China Sea, not at all the kind of consummation he had in mind. Gwenda could no doubt be persuaded (for cash) to cooperate, but he wasn't going down that path again, he'd had

50

enough of Gwenda and her boyfriends. Harriet would scarcely welcome the role of madame, pimp, and mistress of ceremonies. The back of Harriet's car? He was a bit old for that sort of thing, he might sprain a muscle or slip a disk.

He knew one hotel that was comfortable, discreet, and not too choosy. And that was where they ended up. He didn't get back to the Highlanders till 0700 hours Friday morning. There was no mention in the newspapers of the fire at Corriehallie, but he hadn't expected it. It wasn't national news, not important enough. It would make quite an item in the Scottish papers, though, especially the local ones.

Later that morning he rang Emily Broadhill's house near Hastings. A housekeeper told him that Emily was fishing on the Quallar river near Fort Ethelred. Alone, was she? So it seemed.

Farquarson knew most of the Highland rivers, and he knew the Quallar well. A fine prolific west coast river with big runs of summer salmon: fish mostly on the small side, a lot of grilse, but a river worth fishing, great sport, a great challenge. He wondered how familiar Emily was with salmon fishing or the river itself. He knew she was a sporty girl, sometimes riding to hounds, even shooting. But he couldn't recall ever hearing that she was a great angler.

This could lead to a great change of plan.

Perhaps Silver wouldn't be needed at all this time. That would also be an economy.

He could see a fine piece of improvisation here. It would need thinking about. He'd have to do the thinking later because meanwhile he had to think about something else—a speech he was due to deliver at a literary lunch that very day.

Why an admiral should be deemed suitable to address a literary lunch, a gathering of the creative intelligentsia, was a mystery. No doubt some éminence grise, the intended guest of honor, had been struck down with the flu or leprosy at the last moment and in despair they had tried the latest name in the headlines—who else but Admiral Farquarson? Anyway, he had accepted such an invitation for Friday 20, and now found himself sipping gin at 1230 hours among the throng in a gilded banqueting room at the Café Royal.

He had accepted because he had been offered a hundred pounds to speak at short notice, and he looked forward to a free meal and some sport. It also tickled his fancy that this literate gathering had been desperate enough in their quest for a speaker to fall back on a public figure whom they no doubt regarded as a warmongering philistine. He was going to do his best to fill this role—when it came to being a philistine, Farquarson reckoned he should be able to annihilate the competition hands down.

Throughout the meal he ate heartily and chatted cheerfully with his neighbors. He drank brandy through the toastmaster's announcements and the introduction of himself: ". . . victorious commander of the South China War, honor . . . privilege . . . et cetera."

When he stood up to speak he drew a small calculator from his pocket and set it on the tablecloth in front of him, next to his brandy glass. He smiled affably around the room. He intended to try and liven things up a bit.

"My Lords, Ladies, and Gentlemen.

"It is a very great privilege to be invited to address this distinguished gathering. Someone offered me a hundred pounds to come and make this speech, and it looked like easy money. I little expected such a satisfying meal and such bewitching companionship"—and he waved a hand at the aged female on his left, an awesome battle-axe.

Nervous coughs around the room. Apprehension.

"I hold the view that the art of after-dinner speaking, like much of our national life, is mummified, stuck in a rut. The speaker does his painful best, the audience is paralyzed with boredom and hopes only to cheer itself up by finding fault or getting another brandy. You can hardly expect a simple seafarer, accustomed at most to haranguing depraved sailors, to break this hallowed mold in one brief session."

Titters and nervous laughter.

"But still, for better or worse, you will not hear from me the usual bland jocularity in which anything resembling an attempted joke causes the audience to be seized with mirth and hilarity. You will not hear an account of life aboard a warship when we were all young. You certainly won't hear about the South China Sea. You won't even hear the usual old jokes and tags. No, no . . . we must break new ground, visit pastures new, contrive grandiose vistas. What could be more interesting than the comments of an ignorant seafarer on the art to which this luncheon is dedicated? Nothing. So here goes—literature it shall be."

Gasps.

"Apart from the main things—that is, of course, women and money—I have gained much pleasure in life from reading. This leads me straight to the work of Georges Simenon.

"As some reviewers have pointed out, there is nothing especially remarkable in performing the act of coitus ten thousand times in a lifetime. If a man's most active years are from fourteen to sixty-two, that gives forty-eight years of full performance. Knock off a total of, say, three years for illness, accident, polar expeditions, and so on, and there are still forty-five years left. Now, a healthy young fellow should be able to manage once a day at least. So"—he looked at the calculator on the table in front of him and pressed a few buttons—"that makes sixteen thousand, eight hundred and seventy-five bangs in a lifetime, and a splendid thing for fourteen-year-olds to look forward to."

Growls, snorts, deep breathing.

"Now, when it comes to ten thousand *different* women—or, for that matter, sixteen thousand, eight hundred and seventy-five different women—and please don't think I'm being, as they say, 'sexist' about this, it works just as well in reverse—obviously the nature of the proposition changes. Apparently Simenon says eight thousand of them were quickies, so we can really call those ones"—he started working on the calculator again—"the output or product of twenty-two years on the basis of a pure physical count plus energy expended. So that leaves twenty-three years to spare for the other two thousand. This comes out"—more button pressing—"at an average of eighty-seven women per annum, or nearly two a week. This is a far more impressive feat, and even the youngest, most agile and enthusiastic among us must regard it with some awe."

Cries of rage, indignation unsuppressed.

"Should we elect to leave, for the moment, this world of delightful fantasy and dip a toe in the chilly waters of reality, I can mention another writer, an old friend of mine, now dead. I'm not going to name him, but he was most distinguished. He claimed that he, in the course of an energetic life, had possessed twenty-seven women—including, presumably, his three wives. Twenty-seven seems to me a good round number in the circumstances, not so round as fifty-four, but more realistic. I was always exhorting him at least to make it twenty-eight, but he was really past it by

54

then. Now, twenty-seven seems to me an attainable and laudable aspiration for any young man—sights set firmly within the target of possible achievement, none of your Simenon arithmetic for my old friend or for the millions who will emulate him."

Angry shouts now, growing louder. Farquarson cheerfully persevered.

"Having concluded this analysis of the sexual—I mean the literary scene, let me venture further into the lion's den. A plain seafaring man I may be, but when did that ever stop anybody offering an opinion?"

Hoots of anger and derision.

"The son of a friend of mine is being tortured at school by set examinations based on the works of Virginia Woolf and James Joyce. Serves the little bugger right, you may say—with all that sex to look forward to, why *shouldn't* he put up with such dreadful stuff? But *I* say something different. As a Scotsman I say, What's wrong with Burns, James Hogg, Robert Louis Stevenson, George Macdonald Fraser? Where is the virtue in earnestness? Beware, ladies and gentlemen, of earnestness. Tolstoi, Hardy, Hemingway, Waugh, Fitzgerald, Steinbeck—were these pillars of earnestness, I ask? They were not. One way and another these were about as fine a bunch of high rollers as you could meet in a day's march. Joyce could perhaps match them for that—but not, I think, for readability.

"Thank you, Ladies and Gentlemen."

Farquarson sat down to cheers, boos, hoots, catcalls, cries of "sexist," "chauvinist pig," "go back to your boat," "up the Navy," "philistine," "shameless," "fascist," and so on. A large number of people left their seats and marched out of the banqueting room.

Farquarson sat there drinking his brandy and smiling broadly. The rest of the proceedings quickly collapsed into embarrassment and desuetude. Soon he was free to get on with his afternoon's business.

The truth was that Friday afternoon's business, after the escapade at the Café Royal, consisted, first, of going to sleep. He would need all the sleep he could fit in, and the gin and brandy should help. At 1700 hours he awoke and began to consider his plans for Saturday.

He began looking at maps. The whole plan was a gamble, the wildest section of the Grand Design. The trouble was that it looked impossible. He started measuring again, and calculating. *Nothing,* after all, was impossible. Or so they said. Also, it was a two-way switch. If you could achieve what *appeared* to be impossible—then that amounted to an alibi, didn't it? And at this point an alibi might be important.

Speed was the name of the game—had been since he left *Invisible.* If things could be made to move fast enough, confusion would become his friend. That all these things should have happened within this time-scale was obviously impossible. So on—speed—confusion to the enemy.

From London to Fort Ethelred was 490 miles, of which you could call two thirds motorway, or its equivalent. He reached for the now notorious calculator: 326 miles at average 110 miles per hour equaled, say, 3 hours; 164 miles at average, say, 50 miles per hour (for these would be daylight hours, busy roads) equaled about 3½ hours. Total 6½ hours. And why not? The thing was perfectly possible provided the car didn't blow up. It wouldn't matter if the car *did* blow up on the way north, but if something went wrong on the way south, it might take some explaining, depending on what had happened in between, which was itself unpredictable, part of the gamble.

So . . . uproar at Nobb's at 0100, or thereabouts. A nap, time to change, and set off . . . 0400. Arrive Fort Ethelred, say, 1030 hours. Start fishing Beat 3 with Emily—surprise, surprise—at 1130 or earlier. Not a bad time, salmon were often caught at that time of day. After that, things would have to take their course. The trick was to leave, to be back on the road heading south again, by 1400 at the latest. He would like to enter Nobb's around 2000 hours, or not much later. He wanted a good witness then—but there was sure to be someone there, anyway Bertie Varndale was often in the club since his marriage had got into a mess. After dinner he could go to bed earlier than usual, catch up on his sleep.

Having finished with these calculations, he left the club and took a taxi to King's Cross. He meant to hang around and watch the cars arrive for the Edinburgh Motorail; he was certain Colin would travel this way. He kept a good distance from the car-arrival bay, and hung about shiftily behind pillars that were barely adequate to hide him. Eventually he saw them, and it gave him great satisfaction. *Harriet and Colin together.* Well, that had been the object. He wrote down the car number of Colin's decrepit old motor—WAG 100 G. He supposed they'd have been using Harriet's limousine if she hadn't lent it to a lecherous admiral. But that was life—or death.

Another taxi took him back to Nobb's. It was 1930 hours by now and in the smoking room he met Bertie Varndale. Varndale said, "Good evening, Peter. Nice to see you. The evening *Standard* is full of your literary witticisms. You seem to have stirred up quite a hornet's nest. Counting up Simenon's women and dividing them on a calculator—that was a bit thick."

"The idea was to break the mold of British after-dinner speaking."

"It's lucky you've got an admiral's pay. And what will Their Lordships of the Admiralty think about the victorious

57

commander inciting every raw youth in the country to un-counted license, promiscuity, and fornication?"

"Uncounted is what it wasn't. I shall say I was mis-quoted. Anyway, it's what my sailors do. If it's good enough for them, it should be good enough for the rest of the raw youth. As for that literary gang, they include some of the finest fornicators in the country—famous for it. Why should they suddenly become so prim?"

"There's quite a rumpus altogether. They're saying no one has ever put so many feet in their mouth simulta-neously since Spooner."

"I rather enjoyed it," said Farquarson. "Let's get a drink."

He had dinner in the club with Varndale, and later he played bridge.

At 2300 hours a waiter told Farquarson he was wanted on the telephone, an urgent call from Canada. Silver said, "All right for some. Is the car on the train?"

"Bang on," said Farquarson. "Both of them. An old wreck, an Austin, I think. The number is WAG 100 G. Repeat that, please."

"WAG 100 G. It doesn't sound very likely."

"Look, I'm telling you. Spare me the laughs, just do what you're paid for."

"Okay, boss."

"You know the train times? It leaves King's Cross at 2215 hours."

"All under control, boss. But don't forget the ten thousand pounds plus the three hundred. By the way, it didn't half burn. You never saw such a blaze. Good fun, that."

"Well, good luck," said Farquarson. "Will you be in your flat on Sunday afternoon?"

"Why not?"

"Right, see you then. We'll settle up. Provided, of course, that all goes according to plan."

"Right," said Silver. "See you."

He rang off.

Farquarson went back to the card room, where he played late with Varndale, Spengler, and his young enemy Lieutenant West. At 0100 hours Saturday morning, the following hand took place; Farquarson playing as West's partner, the pair vulnerable, West's deal:

NORTH

(Lieutenant West)

♠ A K 10 4
♡ 6
♢ A K Q 3
♣ A Q J 4

WEST

(Lord Varndale)

♠ J 6 5
♡ —
♢ J 10 9 5 4 2
♣ 10 8 3 2

EAST

(Trevor Spengler)

♠ Q 9 7 2
♡ A Q 3 2
♢ 8 6
♣ K 7 5

SOUTH

(Peter Farquarson)

♠ 8 3
♡ K J 10 9 8 7 5 4
♢ 7
♣ 9 6

The bidding:

North	East	South	West
2 ♣	Pass	2 ♢	Pass
2 ♠	Pass	3 ♡	Pass
4 NT	Pass	5 ♣	Pass
5 NT	Double	Pass	Pass
Redouble	Pass	6 ♡	Pass
6 NT	Double	7 ♡	Pass
Pass	Double	Pass	Pass

Farquarson went two down—500 points. There was plenty of room for trouble here. West said, "What's wrong with five no trumps?"

"We go off a pile," said Farquarson. "You can't get at the hearts. It was your stupid redouble that caused the mess. I had to bail you out."

"Five hundred points? Some bail!"

"Look, you play it in five no trumps, sensibly doubled and foolishly redoubled. And what happens? You'll make nine tricks, if you're lucky. So you're down two, vulnerable redoubled. That's a thousand points. Five hundred was cheap."

West had been drinking. He said, "I've had about enough of you altogether. You may be an admiral, but here we're all equal, club members. You always think you're right. In fact, you seem to think you're God, not to mention Nelson."

"Careful," said Farquarson softly.

"Bail me out, indeed. No one really knows the truth about what went on in the South China Sea, do they? Because *you* transmitted so much cock. Lord of the Seven Seas! Try it on the Serpentine, I say. It's like your 'grandiose vistas.' So what were they? Just fucking."

"What's all this about?" asked Varndale.

60

"Look," said Farquarson. "If you want a row you can have one."

"Nothing but bullshit . . ."

Farquarson and West were both standing by now.

". . . to make the bloody Admiral sound like God."

Silence.

Farquarson walked behind Varndale's chair, moved slowly toward West.

"Break it up," said Varndale briskly.

"It's like Grange Hill," said Spengler.

Farquarson took a swipe at West.

West knocked Farquarson stone cold, a fierce right to the chin.

Farquarson came to and looked groggily at his bedside clock. 0400. He realized that he must be in his bedroom at the Highlanders or the clock wouldn't be there. He remembered the fracas at Nobb's. He'd meant to set the alarm for 0400 anyway, but he must still have been unconscious when his chums from Nobb's had carried him to his Highlanders bedroom—at least, he supposed that's what must have happened. Very well. Right. Could he still make it? He thought he could. He had the makings of a fine bruise on his chin but he got out of bed and staggered round, shaving quickly, packing a few things that might be useful—there were still about a hundred Mars bars in the boot of the Jaguar—and dressing in a smart tweed suit.

He scribbled a note, "Gone shopping," and left it on the desk in his bedroom. He hung the DO NOT DISTURB sign—a hangover protection device—on the outside handle of his bedroom door after he'd closed it firmly.

By 0500 the Jaguar was on the motorway, going straight north like a bullet from a high-velocity rifle.

On the early morning radio he heard that he had caused quite a stir. The Saturday national dailies, apparently, were full of Farquarson. From "Curious Address by Admiral," to "China Admiral Exalts Sex," to "Sex—England Expects" to "Aye, Aye, Sir—27 Times" to "Disgraceful Encouragement to Promiscuity," he had evidently cheered up everybody's Saturday-morning reading. He would have been more interested to read the following piece from the Saturday issue of the *Grampian Bugle:*

Most of us thought the Border Wars had ended centuries ago. We thought internecine strife between Highland tribes was a legend of the past. But what happened on Thursday at the Corriehallie Estate in West Grampian was enough to make anyone wonder whether time had advanced at all since the Glencoe Massacre, or Culloden. The lodge itself was burnt to the ground in a blaze so vast that all the Grampian fire-engines within reach couldn't control it. It had pretty well gone, in one huge fireball, even before the first one arrived. Proof that it had been started deliberately was easy enough to come by even if the pace and fury of the blaze hadn't itself been proof positive.

The moors round about were strewn with dead and dying deer. Those of us who have visited this appalling scene could easily believe that a marauding army had devastated the place, spreading bloodshed and destruction. That no human being was injured seems a miracle. A bomb had been tossed into the River Findspey nearby, which is now full of dead salmon.

At the moment no one can think of any possible motive to explain these cruel and apparently insane proceedings. The usual talk about local vandals appears meaningless in the context of the *scale* of these atrocities, also of the fact that the deer were killed by a submachine gun of a type common in certain branches of the army. The bomb—or grenade—in the river appears to have been army issue also. But most such weapons have military origins. A large number of police officers have been deployed in the area, but a police spokesman says it is too soon for any official statement or comment.

Colin Farquarson, the Laird of Corriehallie, is expected to arrive from London this morning to talk to police and examine the wreckage. It is said that he will be accompanied by his ex-wife, from whom he was divorced a year ago.

Farquarson would have been especially interested in the last sentence. What was due to happen next should provide the *Bugle* with food for some more heartfelt indignation.

On the other hand, he might well have been mystified by the headlines above a small column on an inside page that read: "Madman Throws Salmon At Fish-Experts, Local Councillor Gets Black Ear."

It was just after 1130 hours that the Jaguar turned off the public highway onto the private but passable track that ran alongside the Quallar fishing beats. The Quallar was a fine summer river, and the upkeep of such a track was justified so that anglers should not waste good fishing time struggling on foot in heavy waders through heather and bog. Farquarson knew the river well.

His information, based on ringing her Sussex home, was that Emily Broadhill should be fishing Beat 3 today, alone, without a gillie. The Jaguar coasted along the rough track, looking for Emily. Farquarson classified the sisters: Harriet—ritzy; Emily—sporty; Julie—arty. He knew Emily well enough to know that she couldn't do things by halves. Whatever idea she'd got into her head, she would go for it flat out.

He was watching for any human movement, especially some blond hair. Harriet and Julie were both tall and dark, but Emily was a smallish blonde.

By the waterfall pool, which had its own fishing hut on a small mound just above the point where the tail-pool broke away into the rapids, the falls themselves, Farquarson saw a rod propped on a bush. The straight line of a parked rod is easy to pick out against a natural landscape. So where was the lady? Where was Emily?

For a second he could scarcely believe his eyes. Way up—some twenty feet or so above the ground—on a branch of a gigantic larch tree he could see a blond head nodding backward and forward, hair falling to hide the face. She was up on a big branch, kneeling there, arm pumping away with an outsize hacksaw. Evidently there was going to be a change in the landscape.

Farquarson slid the car into the clearing near the hut. For a moment or two he sat and watched the arm pumping away, the saw flashing back and forth in the sun. Something was soon going to fall off—presumably the bough, that seemed to be the idea.

He left the car and made his way stealthily to the shade of the huge tree, close by the water. Now he heard the rhythmic rasp of the saw mincing timber against the murmur of the river, the roar of the falls. He said, "That's a new way of catching them."

The head lifted a little, gray eyes focused down on him. A small neat face, very attractive.

"Peter Farquarson, by God! Come and help me with this. I need someone to pull."

"Pull the other one," said Farquarson.

64

"The branch, you fool. It's almost in half now. A good pull from a beefy fellow like you should get rid of it."

"It's not doing anyone any harm."

"That's where you're *wrong*. How can I fish the pool with this dirty great branch drooping on the water? It's impossible."

"Some of us might not think so. Where did you get the saw from?"

"I borrowed it from the farmhouse. Over there." She pointed, and nearly dropped the saw on Farquarson's head.

"Can't you Spey cast?"

"There's Spey casting and Spey casting," said Emily. "Could you reach it? The place where the fish are, I mean? With the bough still here?"

"Well, yes. It isn't really very difficult."

"God, you're a shit. Grab the branch and heave."

"Are you sitting the right side of it? Like the monkey, I mean."

"Peter Farquarson, I'll kill you. I mean it." She brandished the saw menacingly. "Do something."

Within five minutes the big bough was on the ground near the water's edge. With their joint strengths they managed to drag it a few yards to get it out of the way.

Farquarson looked disparagingly at the rod, parked on its bush.

"What's that thing for?" he said.

"Are you going mad, or am I?"

Farquarson picked it up and whipped it two or three times in the air.

"It's just a toy."

"That is the latest, the most expensive, the very best carbon-fiber—"

"But there's only about nine foot of it."

"Ten," said Emily.

"Do you know anything *about* the Quallar? Well, obviously not. But just *look* at it. At this height, which is

65

below its medium level, it's a huge river. No wonder you need to cut down trees if that's all you've got to fish with."

"You mean *you* couldn't have reached the place where the fish are?" She pointed. "So it wasn't so silly, cutting down the tree?"

"Have you got another rod?"

"Of course not. I can't fish with two rods at once."

"Well, we'll just have to do the best we can with this miserable little stick."

"There's no *we* about it. I rented the river, I bought the rod, I cut down the tree, and now I'm going to catch the salmon. You can take the saw back to the farmer. What are you doing here anyway?"

"I was driving past," said Farquarson. "I thought I'd just like to look in on the Quallar on the way. Memory lane, and all that."

"What's wrong with your chin?"

"The floor came up and hit me."

"You're impossible. Well, I'm going to fish. I didn't cut the tree down just to chat all day with my ex-brother-in-law, even if he has become quite a well-known sailor. You're known in other ways too, I see. My morning paper doth wax indignant about admirals who ought to be setting an example, et cetera, encouraging the youth of the country on to ceaseless and promiscuous sexual endeavor. And I agree with my morning paper. Thank God, you're not my brother-in-law anymore, that's about the only consolation. Now, those salmon had better watch out."

"I'll help you," said Farquarson, "Advice, that's what you need."

"Advice, advice. If there's one thing I hate it's advice. If you won't take the saw back to the farm you can stay and watch—in silence."

She waded in and started casting. Farquarson sat on the bank and watched, grinning broadly. Soon her fly got caught on the tree behind her—a higher branch than the one she had chopped off.

"Bugger," she said.

"That's too high up for me to reach," said Farquarson.

"Shit." She threw the rod into the river in a tantrum and stomped toward the bank. "Do something."

"There's no hurry—it won't go away, will it?" He pointed to where the tip of the rod quivered above the current. "It's still hooked to the tree."

Emily stamped on the shingle with her right foot, quite a difficult thing to do in chest waders.

"Of course there's a hurry. The fish are moving—I've seen them. I'll get away from this bloody tree and try further down, by the falls."

"What with?" asked Farquarson, pointing to the tip of the rod thirty yards away in the water. "We haven't even got the little stick now you've thrown it in the river. You'd better wade out and get it back."

"I think it's too deep now. The current's dragged it out, I can't reach it. I'll climb the tree and I'll—"

"I'll watch that," said Farquarson, grinning, "it should make a most amusing anecdote. But I think you'll have to take your waders off—I don't think you'll be able to get that high with them on. Chest waders aren't made for climbing trees."

"I got up there before."

"But not so high. And even if you get there, you'll have a job to reach the fly."

"You're the kind of Sir Galahad every girl needs. Well, here goes."

"Here's another suggestion," said Farquarson. "We could cut down what's left of the tree, we've still got the saw. That would bring the fly within reach. Then we could pull the rod out of the river by tugging at the wrong end, so to speak."

"That would take all day," said Emily. "I'm going up."

"All right," said Farquarson. "Look. I'll get it for you. Lend me your wading stick/gaff so that I can reach out when I'm up there and get hold of the line."

"Very chivalrous."

"There's one condition, though. Next time you take my advice. It wasn't very bright to get caught up on what's left of the tree—I'd say it was quite difficult, really."

"Shit on you, Peter Farquarson. Get the line—we'll see about the advice later."

Farquarson climbed the tree rather cautiously. It was important to him today that he shouldn't get his tweed suit and country brogues into a mess if he could avoid it. Leaning out on a bough, he reached full-stretch with the long gaff and succeeded in pulling the cast into his hands, thus securing the fly, which he unhooked from a twig of the bough. He could see—what he had guessed earlier—that the fly was too big for the river condition.

"I'll pull it in from up here," he said. "Or near enough for you to wade out and reach it."

A salmon jumped in the far stream.

"Shit," said Emily. "All right, heave away, Admiral. Let's make it quick."

At the end of this pantomime Emily had the rod; Farquarson was back on the ground and he gave her back her wading stick.

"We'll change this fly, for a start," he said, and he did so. "Now," he said, "just above the falls. I'll show you exactly where."

While they were walking the hundred or so yards downstream, first on shingle, then on the steep, grassy bank that followed, Farquarson looked very sharply at the points where the shallow edge of the water lapped against the shingle. Was the river rising? Perhaps a fraction. Good for fishing, good for all sorts of things.

"You wade out precisely here," he said. "For about twenty yards it's quite shallow and the current's not strong enough to worry you. Keep an eye on that white stone on the far bank, that's the wading line. Then you cast the fly, now that you've got the right one, as far as the little stick will let you. Then you should catch something. Have you actually caught any salmon before? In your life, I mean?"

"Lots," said Emily.

"Some salmon are damned unlucky," said Farquarson.

"I could kill you," said Emily.

"Keep it for the salmon. Have a go."

So Emily waded out and began casting as Farquarson had advised. Farquarson sat on the dry grassy bank, which here fell away steeply down to water that flowed about three feet deep. Emily was some twenty yards out, casting away adequately.

Two silver salmon curved out of the water in the center stream, neatly reentering head-first.

"Those could be takers in this water," said Farquarson. "Cast longer. If we had a proper rod, this would be easy."

At this moment Emily's line tightened straight, the rod bent hard over toward the center stream and then jerked twice in response to heavy thuds beneath the surface. She had hooked a salmon.

"Very good," said Farquarson.

Emily began to make a slow and cautious progress toward the bank while allowing the salmon to rip yards of line off the reel in a prolonged scream. This is the classic procedure in these circumstances. When she was standing under the grassy bank, the salmon tearing about and jumping a long way off now, many yards of drowned line, she said, "I can't get up."

"Give me the rod."

"I will not. It's my salmon."

"All right," said Farquarson. "Just stay there, if that's the way you want it. I was going to give you a hand up."

Emily turned her back on him and began to try to control the salmon properly. But she wasn't very successful because she couldn't move about, and she couldn't get up

69

the bank. The salmon kept getting downstream below her. Soon it would be caught in the great sweep of current that led to the falls themselves, and carried away to safety.

"Give me a hand up," said Emily.

"Give me the rod first."

"Shit. All right."

The moment Farquarson had the rod the salmon's chances had lessened. He had height, strength, mobility, and experience on his side. He started to pump the fish away from the falls.

"I need to move down a bit," he said.

"Pull me out."

"There's not time, really. But why not?"

Then everything happened at once.

Farquarson had the rod in his left hand. He bent down and extended his right hand to grasp Emily's right hand and pull her out of the water and up the bank. Their hands met, Farquarson heaved, the salmon jumped, the rod dipped, Farquarson slipped, Emily was jolted and lost her hold of Farquarson's hand. She fell backward into the three feet of water with a great splash and disappeared for a second.

Farquarson concerned himself with the salmon. She couldn't come to much harm there, worse luck.

The next moment she was standing up, very wet, her waders evidently full of water. Too angry to speak, she started to march slowly upstream to a point where the steep bank dwindled away and the shingle began. Access to dry land would be easy there. Farquarson, safe and dry on the bank, moved in the opposite direction, downstream, the better to control the salmon.

By the time she'd got ashore and reached him, the salmon, all glittering sixteen pounds of it, was almost exhausted.

"Here you are," said Farquarson, handing her the rod. "It's your fish, after all. I'll gaff it for you."

"You did it on purpose," she said.

"If I'd been doing it on purpose I'd have found some-where deeper," said Farquarson.

"Tough."

In a few minutes the salmon was safely gaffed.

"A beautiful fish," said Farquarson. "Congratulations. All your own work—well, almost."

"I hate you, Peter Farquarson, and I'm drenched. These things are half-full of water, like flower vases."

"Let's pull them off."

Emily sat down on the grass bank. Farquarson heaved away, and off they came. He tipped the water out of them. The jeans Emily had worn under the waders stuck to her now, sodden and skintight. The sight stirred Farquarson.

"You can't wear those," he said, "you need something dry."

"These are all I've got."

"You can have some of mine. I've got a spare pair in the car."

The car was only about twenty yards away. The fishing hut stood on a little mound covered with heather and moss, between the river and the car.

"Yours will be much too big," Emily said.

"We'll fix them somehow."

"That looks like Harriet's car."

"Well, it isn't," said Farquarson. "Just wait a minute."

The trousers Farquarson brought from the car were ac-tually Silver's, a pair Silver had left there by mistake.

Without her waders Emily had no shoes and she found it too painful to walk in wet socks on the spiky heather. Farquarson lifted her in his arms and carried her easily up the steep little mound to the hut. This stirred him even more.

"I'll help you off with them," he said. "Water sticks them on like glue."

Emily looked him very straight in the face, straight into his eyes, very cool.

"As long as it stops there," she said.

Farquarson grunted and tugged. Emily's short legs were bared to her brief knickers now, the muscles curving and swelling gently—very sexy legs, and gleaming now from their drenching. Farquarson said, "God, I'm feeling randy."

"I warned you," said Emily. "Nothing doing. Your maunderings at the Café Royal have gone to your loins."

"Well, it's all your fault. Seeing those smashing legs, and that smooth rump."

"Give me those trousers. They don't look like yours anyway, they're too small."

"I'll tell you something interesting," said Farquarson, not proffering the spare trousers. "John Wilkes said he could have any woman if he was left alone with her for twenty minutes."

Emily laughed. "Well, you're not doing too well so far. We've been in here ten minutes already, not counting the time on the river. What did he do?"

"Since I wasn't there, I can't tell you. Perhaps he called for madder music and stronger wine. Like the Don. I expect he told them how beautiful they were, how badly they were treated by their husbands, what lovely legs they had and so on, how intelligent they were, et cetera."

"It doesn't sound good enough."

"They say with a stupid woman you should praise her brain and an ugly woman you should praise her body. Perhaps that did the trick, plus the food, the madder music, and the stronger wine."

Emily giggled. "And what will *you* do for food, music, and wine?" She was excited from catching the salmon.

"I've got some Mars bars in the car. Hundreds, in fact. I've got a flask of Scotch, too. So that should be all right. Anyway, kindness is the thing with blondes. You have a beautiful bum."

"That doesn't sound like the language of love to me," said Emily, who was beginning to shake with laughter.

"I daresay he asked them all to marry him, too. That's another well-known method."

"I don't know which method you're using."

"Will you marry me?" said Farquarson.

"Just keep on with the hymn to beauty—more about my bum, for instance."

"Well, you're a very beautiful woman," said Farquarson. "I could go on in that vein for some time—but how's the stopwatch?"

"You won't catch Wilkes."

"The hell with Wilkes. Just feel that now."

"Really, you are the most frightful man."

"I'm much worse than you think."

"The trouble is," said Emily, "you make me laugh."
And she threw her arms round Farquarson and kissed him.

"Perhaps Wilkes made them laugh," said Farquarson.

"Afterward"—as they say in novels, Farquarson said, *"Will* you marry me?"

"Of course not, Peter. I've never heard anything so ridiculous. You made me laugh—we fucked. Now I'm going fishing."

"I've got to go," said Farquarson. "I'll show you a good spot, though. I know this river inside out. We'll go up to the Leopard and I'll show you."

"More advice?"

"You took my advice—you caught a salmon. In the Leopard you might catch five or six, a red-letter day. It's a great pool."

"I saw it. But it's a huge place. I didn't know where to start."

"I'll show you," said Farquarson. "Advice, advice, that's what you need."

When they reached the Leopard, Farquarson said, "Look, you see that silver birch, the one on the right, over on the far bank?"

"Just," said Emily. "It's a long way."

"Don't worry, all this side is slow, shallow water. You wade toward the tree, okay? You keep going for a hundred yards, don't worry if you go up or down the occasional foot or so, it's safe, it doesn't matter. But"—and his voice changed to a harder emphasis, a clearer enunciation—"at a hundred yards there's a shelf. If you cross that you'll probably be drowned. So stop at ninety yards—that's maybe a hundred and thirty paces for a small woman in chest waders. Do you hear me? Repeat it."

"I stop at ninety yards."

"Right, then you're safe on this side of the shelf. Cast as far as you can and even with the little stick you should reach some of them. When you're out there you can tell the wading line from a black rock just off the rapids in the pool below. That's called the Maw, incidentally. Keep on that line and you'll be all right. The real problem out there is if you catch something—it's a bore wading all the way back to the bank and then all the way out again.

"I'm off, then. I'm sorry you won't marry me. But it was a very jolly morning. Tight lines."

"You shit," said Emily, and stepped into the waters of the Leopard to begin the long wade out.

Farquarson watched her for a few seconds before turning away. A sexy figure all right. A waste. But would it work?

The shelf was fifty yards out, of course; everyone who fished the Quallar knew that.

It was risky. There were an awful lot of things that could go wrong; there might even be an accidental witness somewhere, a stray shepherd, someone like that. But the Leopard was a very isolated place. And then—what would

74

they have witnessed? Anyway, if you embarked on a high-risk plan, it wasn't much use becoming a shrinking violet when the risks began to arrive. If Emily *didn't* drown, it would be her word against his. Then people would start asking where he'd been all day. It was a pity, too, that she'd recognized Harriet's car. Never mind, the die was cast, this was no time for faint hearts.

Time pressed. 1330. It was lucky that Emily, what with one thing and another, had been too excited to want to waste time eating lunch.

On his way back to the car he called in at the fishing hut to collect the jeans, still drenched, that he had pulled from Emily's legs.

There was need for haste, and anyway he didn't want to *see* anything happen, he was a bit squeamish.

He tossed the jeans into the boot of the Jaguar, among the Mars bars.

Nobb's called him, and his magic chariot was ready.

At 2000 hours that evening, Saturday, Farquarson strolled into Nobb's.

There was a huge stack of mail waiting for him. While trying for Mach I on the way south, he had heard on the radio that the bomb at Corriehallie had gone off—both parties blown to smithereens, apparently, right outside the gutted shell of the house. Harriet *had* crossed the threshold again, or at any rate bits of her had. The Laird also. It was too soon to expect news of how Emily had fared on the Leopard Pool, anyway it probably wouldn't make national news immediately; not, that is, until someone discovered she was Harriet's sister.

Varndale was in the bar. He said, "I'm sorry about

Colin, old boy. You seem rather accident-prone these days."

"What about Colin? Fought his way into the slammer at last?"

"God, haven't you heard?"

Varndale proceeded to give Farquarson the news he already knew.

"I never liked him much," said Farquarson.

"Someone must have disliked him rather a lot. A bomb, that's what's so extraordinary. It's like Sarajevo."

"It's not at all like Sarajevo. Anyway, Sarajevo wasn't a bomb, though it's what you'd expect with those damned Balkans."

"I suppose that makes you the Laird. At least you'll be better at it than poor old Colin."

"Who wants it?" said Farquarson. "Why was Harriet there anyway? They divorced ages ago, they hated each other."

"Something to do with the wreckage and carnage and arson on Thursday. They decided to travel up together. Apparently there was still a lot of Harriet's furniture in the house. The whole thing's very extraordinary, I must say."

"Let's get a drink," said Farquarson. He summoned the barman.

When they had the drinks Varndale said, "Your life seems to be rather full these days. Winning wars one day, giving scandalous speeches about sex the next, brawling at Nobb's the day after, getting your brother blown up by a bomb the day after that, inheriting Scottish estates, and so on. You can't expect," he went on, "to escape popular attention. How have you been passing the time today?"

"Shopping," said Farquarson. "Well, a woman."

"A woman!" said Varndale. "You're pretty tough, I must say. After West knocked you cold last night and we decanted you in your cozy nook at the Highlanders, you didn't look as though you'd be able to cope with a woman for a week or two."

"I had a good long sleep."

"Everyone's been looking for you, to tell you the terrible news about Colin and Harriet. The news didn't reach London till about noon. Then they went into your bedroom in spite of the DON'T DISTURB sign. But you weren't there. All they found was a note—'Gone shopping.'"

"I couldn't say 'Gone womanizing,' could I? How could I know I was going to be in such demand?"

"You were silly to go for West. You're much older than him and he's a beefy young brute. Fit, too."

"West had been drinking. Anyway, I don't like him, never have. It's an interesting thing, you know. In the service, in the old days, a man hit his senior officer and he was in real trouble—flogging, hanging. Now it's the other way around. Try hitting one of your *juniors* and there's all hell to pay."

"It can't be said you did much in the way of hitting West. You took a swipe at him and he knocked you cold. That's what happened. You've got a fine bruise, too."

"I suppose I ought to challenge him to a duel. That might be fun."

"I'd say you'd had the duel already. You lost. I wouldn't try it again with young West if I were you. Also, as a friend, I'd say your personal publicity is getting out of hand already. A duel between yourself and a young naval gunnery officer who served under your command in the South China Sea is hardly likely to pass unnoticed in the public prints. Then think what this duel of yours will be about. So far as I can make it out, the issue is whether your reports from the scene of battle were one hundred percent accurate. Of course it doesn't matter a damn whether they were accurate or not, we all know that. But you can't fight duels about it. Their Lordships of the Admiralty won't stand for much more of all this, that's my guess. What are you doing this evening?"

It was just as well Varndale knew nothing of Gwenda's letters, which had now assumed a minatory tone. Evidently

Gwenda's prospects were improving. Now she claimed to have an offer of £100,000 from a Sunday paper for her deeply fascinating autobiography, which apparently would be along the lines of Gwenda-Bird Tells of Love Nest with Admiral Humbert Humbert; subtitle, True Sex Life of After-Dinner Speaker.

"Early bed," said Farquarson. "Women are damned exhausting. But what about a spot of bridge first? I saw Jenner and that other chap, Carstairs, in the smoking room. Let's ask them if they'll play after dinner."

"Jenner might not care to play with you."

"Did he complain to the committee?"

"I talked him out of it. Anyway, he'd have made a fool of himself. I daresay I can persuade him to play if you can refrain from multiplying the stakes by ten and from switching declarers after the bidding's finished. You may have to listen to a few jokes about your speech; no one can talk about anything else. It isn't that they've forgotten about old Colin, but it's not as though he'd been a Member."

"Look at this." Farquarson had been opening his mail as they chatted. "Forty-six lots of people have invited me to make after-dinner speeches, everything from the City Guilds to the Portsmouth Officers' Club to the working men's club in Wigan. They don't care what they pay either, it's easy money. The trouble is, I've only got one speech."

"That's the one they want," said Varndale.

The evening passed quietly by Farquarson's standards. He went to bed early to catch up on his sleep. Tomorrow was going to be another busy day.

Sunday afternoon was likely to be busy, since it included the rendezvous with Silver and a later meeting, the culmination of the whole desperate venture. He would have liked to sleep through to lunchtime, but he knew he had to see the morning papers, there was a lot at stake. He was going to find out now what had worked and what hadn't, in particular he was going to find out about Emily. If that part *hadn't* worked . . .

He read the Sunday papers carefully during his breakfast. It had worked all right, everything had worked. "Fishing Sister Drowned." "Laird and Ex-Wife Killed by Bomb." "Violent Deaths of Heiress Sisters." It wasn't the lead in the heavies, but it had caught the imagination of some of the penny dreadful tabloids.

He didn't expect any lawyers to be working on a Sunday—a weird notion indeed—but they were. They must have smelled money. They were on the telephone to him after breakfast about tragedies, wills, insurances, trusts, mortgages, entails, funerals, a whole host of problems concerning Colin and the Corriehallie inheritance. "You will, of course, if I may say so, be visiting the—er—scene of the tragedy? There are certain—um—arrangements."

"I'll go north tomorrow," said Farquarson. "Today's Sunday."

The Emily plan had worked to perfection, that was the real news.

Nearly all the pieces of the Grand Design had now met the destinies appointed for them. One or two loose ends needed to be cleared up, one of them being Silver. Then the final meeting, the final triumph.

He hadn't been dashing around murdering people just for the fun of it.

He spent a lazy morning at Nobb's reading a laughable analysis of the South China War. Really, really.

He lunched with Varndale, who'd had a row with his employers as well as with his wife, and was now in a state of some indignation. None of it really mattered; Varndale had stacks of money and was widely liked and respected. It was evidently his pride, the principle of the thing. He said, "Stockbrokers, city men, that's different. They're speculators, the casino bit. Nothing wrong with that, except that it's mostly rigged. It's a form of 'inside' dealing, but how inside is inside, that's the question. Still, they take risks, however slight, of losing money, sometimes even of going to jail, though in practice neither of these things ever seems to happen. Never mind. Risks are taken, decisions are made, the pagoda tree shakes and down falls a thousand tons of gold bullion. Fair enough—well, almost.

"But *management*—that's different. Management doesn't—individually or even collectively—do *anything* except bugger up the people who are trying to do the job, manufacture the product, whatever it may be, engineers, textiles, electronics. You get the odd exception—Michael Edwardes, for instance—but that's really a political thing, or possibly a leadership thing, though it's fashionable to pretend it's management.

"Any average competent fellow, reasonably sensible and educated, could run almost any medium-size business single-handed in his sleep. You don't need to be a Henry Ford who *created* the thing. But he must have the power to do one thing—fire all the management in sight. Then he has to bribe or bully the unions. After that, it's just a question of getting the right workers and letting them work, knowing the names of their wives, and all that. Then it will run itself. The more people you have arguing about figures at meetings, the less gets done and the more it costs. Sack them all and get on with it, that's what I say."

"Management is rubbish," said Farquarson.

While Farquarson was planning his afternoon visit to Silver, a meeting of police chieftains was taking place in the central Highlands.

On Sunday the twenty-second the Chief Constable of Dornoch met the Chief Constable of Nevis in the police station of a small town that lay between their respective fiefs. They were accorded the Chief Inspector's office to themselves, and there they sat, either side of the desk, while the morning August sun burned down outside.

Sir Terence Vraismouth from Dornoch was musta-chioed, bristling, and angry. He said, "This is a hell of a mess. I've got a dead Laird and his ex-wife, both blown to bits. You've got the ex-wife's sister, also dead. I've also got a lot of dead deer and salmon, and an incinerated mansion. The fact that they were sisters must mean something. But what?"

Sir William Toothboy from Nevis, gaunt and reserved, said, "Cui bono? I know the law pretends motive doesn't matter much, but policemen think of motive first. Who's actually gained, or will gain, anything?"

Sir Terence said, "Peter Farquarson inherits Cor-riehallie. But who the hell *wants* Corriehallie? No one in their right mind, not Peter. These sisters had a stack of money—inherited it from their father, that old rogue who ran crook car auctions all round Glasgow. My men have been on to the London lawyers, and guess what?"

"I'm listening," said Sir William.

"These shit lawyers in London—they're so damned disjointed. They have plummy voices and keep on saying things like 'If I may say so,' but their minds aren't on it. At least, not the part of their minds that deals with trusts and law. They charge twenty guineas for five minutes. So they're watching the clock in front, counting the minutes, writing down the guineas. Naturally they can't worry about *legal* business, they're like middle-aged counting boys—minutes, guineas, that's all! That's lawyers—I hate 'em."

"No one likes lawyers," said Sir William coldly. "But they must have told you *something.*"

"Well, they don't know. 'It might be construed . . .' 'within the discretion of the trustees . . .' 'a court might take the view . . .' 'an interpretation of clause eighty-three of Mr. Morrison's will . . .' and so on, and so on, guineas, guineas, guineas!" Sir Terence banged furiously with his fist on the table. "Bastards! Guinea pigs!"

"Is that really all?"

"Yes, just about. Now, common sense, that's different. Mrs. Farquarson died first, so the doctors say. So the money goes to Mrs. Broadhill, right? Mrs. Broadhill dies next, having inherited, an hour or so earlier, from her sister. So now it's two great stacks of money in one. Now this great stack is inherited by either Miss Morrison, aged thirty-nine, last of old Morrison's line. Or by Victoria Broadhill, Emily Broadhill's daughter. That's where the guinea pigs get so vague and disjointed. Anyway, what the hell? Miss Julie Morrison was at a health farm until yesterday evening, and very young Miss Broadhill was with friends in Deauville. So that about cui bonos it."

"What about Farquarson?"

"Peter Farquarson has almost no motive and masses of alibi. In the steps of his late lamented brother, he seems to have been brawling and gambling almost every evening around St. James's Street—none of your old strip joints and knocking shops for him, the very best of S.W.1., you name it."

Sir William Toothboy grew colder and more withdrawn

82

as Vraismouth grew more purple and exasperated. "But *could* he have been mixed up in any of it?"

"Probably not. Certainly not with Emily Broadhill. Anyway, she fell in the bloody river, didn't she? What's that got to do with Farquarson, even if he could have been there, which it seems he couldn't?"

"The Leopard and the Maw. That's a funny thing."

"Not so funny as telling the public that the Commander in Chief of the South China War is helping police with their inquiries. That would be even funnier," said Vraismouth, purple and puffing.

"Did you see what Farquarson was up to on Friday? His speech in London?"

"I did."

"I think he's going off his head."

"Did you actually *read* the speech?" asked Vraismouth.

"Of course not. I've got other things to do than waste time studying the maunderings of admirals at writers' beanos."

"Well, I've read it. The point is, it's a joke. All the howls of rage, anguish, indignation, et cetera, have buried the reality, which is that Peter Farquarson was making a joke. Apparently everyone wants him to make speeches now."

"A costly joke—for him," said Toothboy.

"I wouldn't even be sure of that. Jokes often *are* costly for the people who make them, I've noticed that. But who would live without jokers?"

Toothboy said, "What was the fifty-four business?"

"So you have read it," said Vraismouth. "I might have guessed. That was a joke too."

"I don't understand it—it's not very funny."

"Dead right it's not. In fact, it's what they nowadays call 'deeply discounted,' in this case so damned deep that you can hardly see it at all."

"I couldn't see that any of it was funny."

"Nor me," said Vraismouth. "The point about the speech being a joke is only that the speech was a joke. It doesn't have to be funny. The trouble all comes with this business of egging on every male under the age of ninety to ceaseless seduction and sexual enterprise. But as they were all doing that anyway, I can't really see what the fuss is all about."

"Well, I *can*. What about Farquarson's reputation—it can't have done that much good."

"The trouble with Peter is that he doesn't seem to care anymore."

"How did he get to be an admiral?" asked Toothboy.

"A form of self-control, I guess. Plus ambition. Anyway, it was only a speech, it's not like rape or murder."

Toothboy said, "I can't make out this business about the house and the deer and the salmon. Didn't anyone *see* anything? People? Cars? Someone must have seen something."

"It's isolated. Very tumbledown too, sort of abandoned. A young man who sounds like a pretty tough customer tried to sell some salmon to our local fish experts in the market. True to form, they tried so hard to swindle him that they overdid it."

"What do you mean?"

"Well, he lost his temper and threw them at them— that is, he threw the salmon at the fish experts. He hit one too, old McGregor. He's got a black ear now. He's a town councillor."

"I find all this very hard to believe," said Toothboy.

"In this world you believe what you believe."

"How did he manage for transport?"

"He had an old Land Rover. Very old."

"Where did that come from? Did anyone know about it?"

"*Everyone* knew about it. It's been in a barn at Corriehallie for twenty-five years. The only surprise was that anyone could make it go. It wasn't licensed or insured—you wouldn't expect marauders and cutthroats to bother with trivia like that. Then, from a distance, someone saw a young man, who might or might not have been the same young man, along with another clown—a literal clown, if you can stand any more of this—dressed up like a Victorian butcher, straw hat and all, great red beard. Either they're all going mad or I am," puffed Vraismouth.

"Could that have been Farquarson?"

"It *could* have been anyone, couldn't it? Neptune, Muhammad Ali, Sheikh Yamani, the Yeti. I can't conceive that it was Farquarson. Why on earth would he dress up like that?—It all seems so crazy. Now tell me about this horrible river of yours, how it drowns people."

"It drowns about two people a year," said Toothboy. "The pool called the Leopard is a long wade out in chest waders so that you can cast out to reach the place where the fish lie under the far bank. It's a tough wade for a woman anyway. It's all right for a strong man, provided he knows where the shelf is. You see, once you've waded fifty or sixty yards out without any trouble, you get a bit over-confident. It all seems safe and simple. The shelf is about fifty yards out in low or medium water. You can't wade the place at all in high water. But if you're walking steadily along, getting more confident and closer to the fish, and if you just happen to walk over the shelf into twenty feet of swirling current—well, you get swept away."

"Where to?" asked Vraismouth.

"The Maw—the pool just below."

"Then what happens?"

"Then you get drowned," said Toothboy. "That's a very bad place, a mass of fast whirlpools, and deep. If you get swept from the Leopard to the Maw, you drown, even if you're young and strong."

"Didn't this silly woman *know* the river?"

"No. She'd never fished it before."

"Where was the gillie?"

"They don't have gillies there anymore. I keep telling them they should, but they won't."

"It sounds like an accident to me," said Vraismouth.

"Yes." Toothboy was silent for a few seconds. "And yet . . . well, there were traces of someone else on the beat that day, footsteps on the bank, scuffed sand on the floor of the fishing hut . . . *something* wrong. . . . And the wrong trousers."

"Someone pushed her in?"

"She might just have been misdirected, I suppose."

"Who have you in mind?"

"I'd like to know more about Farquarson's alibi."

"You've got Farquarson on the brain. What the hell did *he* stand to gain by encompassing the end of Mrs. Broadhill?"

"I'd still like to know about his alibi."

"I'll get it checked again, but I think you've got Farquarson on the brain. There's something else—a car's disappeared. The late Mrs. Farquarson owned a new Jaguar XJS, special version, umpteen thousand pounds. But they went to Corriehallie—and got blown up—in some old banger of the Laird's. No one can find the Jaguar. Not that it means much to me—none of it means much to me, or to my detectives. Then . . . well, look at this. Goodness knows where the time-and-tilt thing came from, but what was the *point* of it? I mean, it could perfectly well have been set in London. It makes no sense at all for Farquarson to arrange a lot of London alibis and then use a toy which can be set in London—which means he doesn't have to go anywhere near Corriehallie anyway. If you think about it, this just makes more of a muddle than ever. Also it makes me think your ideas about Farquarson are rubbish. And what's this now about the wrong trousers?"

"Mrs. Broadhill's body, when it was pulled out of the river, didn't have her own jeans on. She was wearing a man's trousers, which is completely inexplicable since she wasn't a transvestite. And even if she had been, what would be the use underneath chest waders? It's something else my men don't understand."

"What's happened to her own trousers—jeans, or whatever?"

"If we knew that, we'd know a lot more than we know now."

"Whose trousers were they? The ones she was wearing? These trousers sound important to me. It's the first I've heard of them."

"We don't know. And since they're just mass supermarket issue we're not very likely to find out."

"Is this why you've got Farquarson on the brain?"

"These trousers," said Toothboy, "are much too small to fit Farquarson."

"I should forget about Farquarson," said Vraismouth. "We've got enough problems without concoctingg demented theories, or nursing crazed obsessions."

"Just check his alibi for my corpse—for Emily Broadhill."

On this note the police chieftains parted, going their separate ways in luxury limousines.

In his bedroom at the Highlanders Farquarson held the Bulgarian pellet in the palm of his hand.

It was time for his visit to Silver, and there was no doubt this would be uncertain, risky, maybe even downright dangerous. He had checked by telephone in the morning that Silver would be at home in his Soho flat for the afternoon rendezvous they had originally planned.

Even the weather was running Farquarson's way, his

luck seemed to be in. After a fine, warm night, the morning had brought a heat shower, a pretext for the umbrella that was to be the tool or weapon on which destiny hinged. Any fool could see it wasn't likely to rain again, England was in the center of a high anticyclone. If it hadn't been for the heat shower, Silver might well have cast a suspicious eye on the umbrella—what could Farquarson be doing with it in such weather? What was it for? Silver might still think it a bit odd, but the heat shower would have made it perfectly plausible. There could be another.

Farquarson looked at the pellet. He didn't know what the hell the Bulgarians did, but he had bought a tube of superglue. With this he carefully stuck the pellet to the point of an umbrella that he had stolen from the cloakroom at Nobb's.

Presumably you had to be careful not to touch the pavement. That would break the pellet and might even do a mischief to any passing dog, cat, lemur, or barefoot child, if there were still any of such people around. He'd have to carry the thing on his arm, swinging it cheerfully like an Edwardian rake with his malacca cane. It would be safest to shoulder arms, but that would be absurdly conspicuous. He rolled the umbrella carefully, less conspicuous, minimum wind resistance.

Was there any risk that the superglue would defuse the pellet in some way—an obscure and uncovenanted chemical reaction? It didn't seem very likely.

He left the Highlanders and strode through the afternoon sunlight on his way to Soho, cheerfully swinging the umbrella.

Farquarson realized that the death of Silver was not likely to pass unremarked. Apart from the police, there would be the press. "Soho Hit Man Slain By Bulgar Brolly" was the stuff of dreams for tabloids; all that, plus a name like Silver, add in Jonathan's reputation and stir, and you would have a *bombe surprise* all right.

But Farquarson was concentrating on the immediate

business, which was to murder Silver. He was concentrating on the umbrella, too, the means to that end. He wasn't too worried about what would happen afterward because he couldn't see any way in which he could be linked to the forthcoming event, provided he was careful. He'd been very choosy about which umbrella he stole, this kind were three a penny. Provided he was careful, there was no way his name could even be thought of in connection with Silver—unless Silver had been talking, and that didn't seem likely either.

In his left hand he carried the large rectangular briefcase in which the ten thousand pounds were sandwiched. The idea was not to part with this money, but there might come a moment when he would have to pretend that he was going to do so.

He walked down the basement steps at the appointed time, half past three, 1530 hours.

Silver was not this time *en deshabille*. Far from it, he seemed to be parceled up in towels that looked like togas, swathed from neck to ankle. Today he was a real little thug, none of your feline engagingness. In fact, he seemed to have so many clothes on that Farquarson wondered where would be the best place to prod with the umbrella when the time came.

Silver let Farquarson into the big sitting room with the pornographic blowups.

"Let's sit down," said Farquarson. He hung the umbrella carefully over the back of one of the two chairs that were drawn up at the big round table. When he had sat down on this chair the umbrella handle was just below his right shoulder, and behind it. It wasn't the ideal position from which to grab it at short notice, but no doubt an opportunity would arise for some movement as time went on. Silver sat down in the other chair.

"Aren't you a bit hot in all that gear?" said Farquarson hopefully.

"Yes," said Silver.

"Wouldn't you like to take some of it off?"

"Yes."

Farquarson was puzzled as well as frustrated. He said, "Why don't you then?"

"It's a fitness thing. Sweating, like a Turkish bath."

"It is a bit pongy in here, now you mention it."

"I didn't mention it," said Silver. "Where's the cash?"

"In the bag here." Farquarson pointed at the briefcase by his feet.

"Plus the three hundred pounds?"

"No," said Farquarson. "You owe me for the fish."

"Look, boss, that was seventeen pounds, ninety-four pee. We're talking about money."

"It's not possible. They can't have swindled you as bad as that."

"They was bad fish, boss. Crook Scots."

"There was nothing wrong with the fish. Even I could have got forty quid or so for them. I knew those fish swindlers would skin you, but *that*—seventeen pounds, ninety-four pee—it's ridiculous."

"It's not a laughing matter."

"Oh yes, it is," said Farquarson. "It's what you'd expect, I suppose. A simpleminded young fellow stuns a few score of salmon with a bomb, carts them off to our local fish experts—then he gets swindled. What else could happen?"

"Well, I didn't accept it. I know when I'm being done."

"What happened to the salmon then?"

"I slung them at them."

"Really? All at once or one by one?"

"Look, boss, salmon is slippery. It was one by one, that was hard enough."

"Did you hit anyone?"

Silver grinned. "I just did. There they were, hiding under their stalls, sheltering behind street corners. They were greedy for the fish but frightened of getting an earful. One was greedier than the others and he *did* get an earful."

"You didn't tell me about all this before."

"Why should I? Who likes to be swindled?"

"It must have been a delightful scene," said Farquarson, "it should have made a most amusing anecdote. I'm sorry to have missed a thing like that."

"Are you laughing again?"

"Well, yes," said Farquarson. "I wish I'd seen that."

"It was your *brother.*" Evidently this had shocked Silver.

"Well, yes," said Farquarson cheerfully. "Worse things happen at sea. Much worse, actually."

"You blew up your own brother?"

"Strictly speaking, it was you who blew him up. Either way, he can't be put together again. *Que sera, sera.*"

"But that's about what's *going* to happen. I know that bit, it's the same as 'Whatever will be, will be.' It isn't about what happened yesterday."

"Viewed in the great dimensions of time and space, I don't suppose it makes a lot of odds," said Farquarson airily. "Let's get back to the fish."

"You've been making speeches, I see." Evidently Silver wasn't at all pleased about the fish joke. "There are a lot of rumors about you, and I could add to them, couldn't I? Arson, multiple murder, and so on. I don't understand about Mrs. Broadhill."

"You don't understand about anything," said Farquarson, "and you don't need to."

"I reckon you did me out of ten thousand pounds there."

"Do you?"

Farquarson was exercised about the umbrella. Was it balanced right, positioned so that he could grab it quickly? How thick were Silver's socks? That seemed to be the only gap in his armor, so to speak. He would have to move

91

pretty quickly when the time came; it was vital to surprise Silver—that, indeed, was the whole point of the pellet. If he failed to surprise Silver and aim straight at the best spot, there'd be problems, big problems. Silver was younger, tougher, and quicker than Farquarson, and just as ruthless.

Also he was getting restless. Here they were, chatting away like old comrades-in-arms, and the umbrella wasn't in an ideal position. What was needed was some movement.

"Get me some of your arrack," said Farquarson, "the Black Label, that is. Parting with all this cash makes me feel ill."

"I haven't had a glimpse of it so far. How do I know you've even got it?"

"There's not much you can do if I haven't."

"Isn't there?" said Silver.

"Anyway, it's in the bag, I told you." Farquarson kicked the big briefcase by his feet. "Get me a drink."

"As you say, boss."

While Silver was pouring drinks, Farquarson surveyed the room carefully, noting especially the corner where Silver left stray armaments lying about.

Then he reached behind him for the umbrella, raised it, and aimed it like a shotgun toward the upper window, where feet could be seen treading along the pavement outside. Silver said, "That's not a swordstick, is it?"

"Would I be aiming it like a gun if it was?"

"That's logical. What's the idea, blowing the feet off birds?"

"Dreaming of capercaillie," said Farquarson.

"Don't pull the Highland bit with me. I've had enough of the bloody Highlands for one whole lifetime. It was terrible in that forest. Mars bars and raw trout—that's bad grub, boss."

"What happened to your rations?"

"They were eaten by a dog."

"You'll be kicked out of the Brownies next. I don't believe you, either. You're supposed to be trained, battle-hardened, a professional survivor. And you let a *dog* eat your rations? Come off it."

"Truth is, boss, I forgot them."

"That's more like it. You're used to having all these things laid on for you, part of the logistics. Left to yourself, you can't even remember to take any food. I couldn't understand it—anyone would think the dog would have preferred the trout and the Mars bars, given the choice."

"You must be joking," said Silver. His last words.

"Where's the drink? It's taking a long time coming."

Now Farquarson was swinging the umbrella casually, its handle in his right hand. He should be able to get a good grip quickly if Silver came close enough.

Silver carried a tumbler of Scotch in one hand and a water jug in the other. He came close to the table, where Farquarson still sat.

Farquarson stood up, tripped over the briefcase, slipped. Having contrived all this while Silver's hands were full, he drove the umbrella like an assegai, full force into Silver's sock. He could feel it strike flesh—and penetrate it too.

Silver screamed, dropped the tumbler and jug, gripped the edge of the table for support.

Farquarson rolled away into the corner of the room where the guns were. Silver just might fancy the idea of some gunplay. But if what Farquarson had read about the pellets was true, there shouldn't be much time left for Silver at all, at all.

Silver turned blue and fell squirming to the floor, making dreadful noises. He wouldn't squirm long, thought Farquarson, who began to search the flat.

He needed to be quick, but it was worth having a look. Maybe some of the earlier money was lying around somewhere, he might as well recoup all he could. It wouldn't pay for the new house at Corriehallie—someone else was going to do that—but it might help pay to make a start on the cellars.

He found a few thousand pounds, which he stuffed in his pockets—the briefcase, which he was going to take away with him, was already jam-packed. Then he carefully cleared away every trace of his presence, and wiped the umbrella especially carefully.

He was going to leave it to amuse the police and the press.

He walked back from Soho. At the Highlanders he unloaded all the cash from the briefcase and from his pockets into a locked drawer in his bedroom. There wasn't much doing at the Highlanders on a Sunday, but a skeleton staff at Nobb's provided him with tea and muffins. Later he had a gossip and a drink or two with Varndale. Then he caught a cab to Hampstead.

For a moment he paused to look at the outside of the Victorian house, long since converted into luxury flats. It was here, in a handsome double bed, that the Grand Design had been conceived. Nothing else had been conceived in that bed, but not for lack of activity; it had been deliberate, a policy of expediency. And now it had all come true.

Julie's flat was on the first floor. Farquarson didn't need to use the buzzer, he had his own key. A punctual man, he let himself in at almost exactly 1830 hours and strode up the stairs—he had always scorned the lift—to Julie's flat, to which again he had a key.

Julie Morrison was tall and dark, as Harriet had been,

but younger, smoother, a little shorter and full-bodied.

The flat faced east, the evening sunlight didn't fall on the windows. One of the two tall standard lamps in the drawing room was lighted to help Julie with her work. She was on all fours on the floor, bent over and working on a huge needlework pattern of tea-clippers in full sail. She wore blue jeans and a white cashmere roll-top sweater. Her dark hair flopped long and straight around her face as she looked up to see Farquarson enter. He could feel his loins working—once again.

She got to her feet, straightened, and walked toward him.

They kissed.

Farquarson saw she had been crying. He noticed too that there was no passion in the kiss. This passion they had shared for over two years—and this was no moment to lose it. He looked into her brown eyes and said, "What's wrong?"

"Everything."

She said, "I tried to tell you. I tried to stop you. It was all a mistake."

"Was it?" said Farquarson.

"I never meant it, I didn't want it at all, I tried to reach you."

"You knew where to find me."

"*No one* knew where to find you. Anyway, I thought you'd come to see me before you did anything. I meant to tell you. Poor Harriet . . . poor Emily."

"How was the health farm?" said Farquarson.

"I didn't worry while I was there. You were still at sea, a week ago. I thought you'd come and see me *first*, before you did anything."

Farquarson said, "We planned—right?—we planned together that you would spend that particular week at a health farm for your own safety—a perfect alibi. While you were there, *I* was to carry out what *we* planned. Correct?

Come on, darling, cheer up, get some champagne out. We need a sense of victory, triumph, ecstasy. Now's the time to celebrate. We've done what we wanted—we've got it— now we enjoy it."

"But I never *meant* it."

"Oh, come on, old thing. Champagne. You'll soon cheer up. All the money plus Corriehallie—as we planned. We've got it. We've arrived. Think of the fun we'll have. We'll build a sweet Westphalian home, a palace in Ecuador, a castle in Scotland. We'll have healthy brats chasing birds across the moors, fishing crystal burns. And they haven't got a chance of catching me—us. There's not much they could do if they *did*, come to that."

"I can only think of Harriet and Emily. Did you *have* to make that speech at the Café Royal?"

"It was a joke," said Farquarson. "A *divertissement*, as they say."

"Twenty-seven! It's disgusting. And I'm just one . . ."

"Look. Think. Are you unhappy because your sisters have come to grief or because I made a joke after-dinner speech? You plotted it about your sisters, we planned it together, before I went to the South China Sea. That was the Grand Design. And you can't be serious about the Café Royal—you just can't, you're Julie, not a half-wit reporter."

"I was wrong. You were wrong. We were wrong. It was completely wicked. And now *you* treat it like a joke."

"Oh no, I don't," said Farquarson. "Not at all, I don't. But what's all this *about?* It was planned ages ago, we both knew what we wanted."

"I've changed," said Julie. "It was that damned speech . . . no, it wasn't really, it was the whole thing, the wickedness."

"Get me a drink," said Farquarson.

They sat apart in huge armchairs separated by the tea-clippers. Both the two tall standard lamps were now alight, and daylight fell through the big window that faced east.

Farquarson took a good swig at his glass and said, "What happens now? Do we lose each other *now?* I shall never understand women."

"That wasn't the impression you gave at the Café Royal."

"Look, for God's sake, which is it? Your sisters—well, *tampis,* who plotted it, you and me, right? Or a bit of sport among the assorted literati?"

"What about that wretched girl you keep in Chelsea?"

"Kept. How do you know about her?"

"Harriet told me—just the other day."

"Very careless of Harriet. People should be more careful about chatting to other people who are planning to murder them."

"Kept?" said Julie. "She's finished with?"

"She's trying to sell her story to a Sunday paper. One hundred thousand pounds. What's so interesting about her sex life I can't imagine, but that's the way it goes."

"What's interesting is *you.* Aren't you worried? You should be."

"Not the slightest," said Farquarson. "She's just a little slut."

"A rich little slut."

"Peanuts," said Farquarson. "Everyone will have forgotten it in a week. And where will she be after that? Some lout will marry her for her money—the heiress—and it will all be spent inside a year. Then the revenue will turn up with a bill for fifty thousand pounds. That should make the basis for a happy marriage, years of solid bliss, graceful old age, and so on. It serves her right."

"What about your old age?"

"I thought we had all that planned."

"You always win, is that it?"

"That's the idea," said Farquarson. "It surprised the wogs, all right."

"Jonathan Silver came to see me," said Julie.

"Did he? When?"

"This morning. He's more intelligent than you think."

"Is he?" said Farquarson.

"He spotted what you were up to."

"Did he?"

"He's not the fool you think."

"Do I?"

"He's quite a man."

"Is he?"

"I took to him."

"To *Silver?*" said Farquarson.

"He's more my age."

"He's fifteen years younger than you. You're twelve years younger than me. And he's about half your height. Did I tell you the story about the naked dwarfs?"

"For God's sake, Peter!"

"It was this loony in Hastings. He chased after naked dwarfs with a camera—a sort of poor man's Lewis Carroll."

"Where did he find any naked dwarfs in Hastings?"

"I don't think he did, really. I expect it was all in the mind."

"Is that the whole story?"

"I suppose so," said Farquarson.

"It's not a very good story," said Julie. "We were talking about Jonathan Silver, who is *not* a dwarf."

"No," said Farquarson. "But he's not in very good shape."

"What do you mean? . . . You don't mean to say . . . it's not possible." Julie's febrile surface manner seemed now on the point of disintegration. "Have you killed Jonathan too?"

"He's not in very good nick."

"Of course, I should have seen it, it was obvious. And now no one knows about it at all except me."

"That was how we planned it," said Farquarson.

"You can say that. But I was never *serious* about it. We joked in bed—we were in love. At least I thought we were. And *this,* Peter, is the real point. These dreadful things have been done, and they can't be undone." She was in tears again. "But *you've* changed, you've become different to *me,* can't you see?—a different person. If I agreed to any of these things, it was because I loved you as I believed you to be, I wanted you, I'd do anything to keep and hold you. But now I see you *differently.*"

"Did you think murdering your sisters was just a jolly jape?"

"I was in love, out of kilter, mad. But the person I loved didn't exist. I never thought you'd *really* kill anybody, in any case I meant to stop you. I can see you've got a case, an argument that we agreed all this, but—"

"I've got more than a case," said Farquarson grimly. "I've got tapes."

"You taped our talks in my bed?"

"That's right."

"You shit." Julie was recovering now, she'd always had lots of spirit, another thing Farquarson liked. "That shows *your* love for *me* in a true light. As does the bint in Chelsea. As does the speech. As do the other twenty-six, or fifty-four, or a thousand and three women, or whatever number it really is. I was in love with . . . an . . . ogre."

"It's no use carrying on like that," said Farquarson. "What's done is done. It's a question of what happens next. Perhaps you'd better sleep on it—you're a bit upset. We might even sleep on it together."

"Never again," said Julie. "Never, never. You really are the most frightful man. To think that I was going to *marry* you—I was mad, still am a bit crazy, but in a different way. There's something else, too. . . . What would *my* life be worth after I'd married you? By marrying me you'd get all the money you're so keen about. Then the money gets spent on Corriehallie, doesn't it? That's the whole idea. By that time I might become unnecessary, even dangerous, like Jonathan. And people fall into *rivers,* Peter, don't they? . . . Poor Emily."

Farquarson said, "Really, in this world, when it happens that two plus two make five, or that a square is not a circle—"

"I won't stand it." Julie's voice was loud and high now, not a cry or a scream, not even a shout, but clear and desperate. "I can't bear it. It's not standable. No one could stand it. I used to think some of it was funny before these dreadful, awful crimes were done. But now—it's too much, it's not bearable. Circles, squares, dud sums, naked dwarfs, all the rest of it, how *can* I stand it, how could *anyone* stand it!"

She broke into great heaving sobs, tears streamed down her face.

"I'll come back on Tuesday," said Farquarson. "I've got things to do. Think carefully, though, when you're a bit calmer. Remember—I don't like being cheated, I like to win. Anyway, it's a toss-up what those lawyers say."

"I don't know what you mean."

"It means that I'll see you on Tuesday," said Farquarson.

But in fact they would never meet again. The Grand Design had foundered.

On Sunday evening the Highlanders Club was closed except for the use of its bedrooms, and there wasn't much going on at Nobb's. In the absence of a weekday staff at Nobb's, he had to harry the night porter to get him a large Scotch and soda at 2330 hours. At midnight he left, telling the porter he was going back to his bed at the Highlanders.

Then he drove the Jaguar down to Beachy Head, stopping only once on the way to steal a hefty piece of breeze block from a building site. He took the opportunity to dispose of Emily's still sodden jeans: he extricated them from among the Mars bars and dumped them in a skip.

He had finished with the car now. It had done all that could be expected of it. But it might have left some traces of its presence at various times and places. Indeed it might well have picked up and be carrying with it telltale proof of its adventures. Even with the naked eye, bits of peat could be spotted around the wheels. It had become a danger to him. And what better than high cliffs, a vertical drop, a deep, tidal ocean?

Farquarson knew the scrub around Beachy Head was populated by coast guards, police, samaritans, and so on, people devoted to preempting tragedy, or—when that didn't work—to rescue. But this wasn't going to be a tragedy, just a heap of expensive, bent metal. The logic was that organizations designed to preempt or alleviate tragedy wouldn't succeed in interfering with a non-tragedy, something in its nature different.

There was a high moon over the cliffs. The Jaguar didn't exactly shine in the moonlight, being caked now with mud and spray and diesel mist.

He lined the car up, bonnet pointed straight toward the cliff edge, steering wheel centered so that the wheels exactly paralleled the car, aiming ahead.

No one would notice the additional noise of another car engine. The Great British public, filled with energy and flush with cash as usual, had been tempted away from their porno-videos by the high summer night, the thrilling moonlit view, and the hope of seeing a few suicides. Even at that hour, about 0200, there were cars everywhere, advancing, reversing, turning in and turning away, headlights blazing. There were even screaming children and yapping dogs. The

101

sound of another car engine was just going to be the sound of another car engine, whichever direction the car was aimed in. It was the splash that counted.

The car's automatic was in the "Park" position. The engine ticked over gently. Farquarson stood by the driver's door, which was half open. The handbrake was off, indeed the car would have slid backward, away from the cliff edge, if the "Park" hold hadn't been on. Now was the moment.

He whisked the gear handle from "Park" to "Drive," dropped the breeze block on the accelerator, slammed the door.

The huge car raced forward, straight for the edge of the cliff. Then it soared and spun away into the velvet night. Engine racing and hiccuping, it twirled downward and away. The Mars bars in the boot would be whizzing around like angry insects. It struck the sea with a tremendous splash.

The splash did it. From the scrub nearby sprang policemen, coast guards, samaritans, St. John's Ambulance men, boy scouts, divers, climbers, stretcher-bearers, a small army. But of course they weren't looking for Farquarson, they were thinking of the man or woman or both who had so ardently sought a leaky coffin, suicides who had escaped preemption but who might yet be rescued.

Farquarson found it easy to melt away in the confusion. They weren't looking for people *outside* the car— that would be a break with tradition, very eccentric. They were looking for people *inside* it. And long would they look, it was high tide now, Farquarson had planned it so.

Through the balmy night he strolled across the downs, past Belle Tout, Birling Gap, up and down the Seven Sisters, seven miles to Seaford. At about 0400 hours on Monday morning he presented himself at a decaying hotel on the Seaford seafront, a place called the Esplanade. The night watchman proved to be a harridan of demonic demeanor, half as old as time. She was encased in a kiosk in the vestibule that someone had chosen to adorn with two great chunks of conical rock, one on either side; these looked like pieces that had fallen off a very early statue by Henry Moore, about 200 B.C.

"I want a bed," said Farquarson.

"This is a respectable house," said the harridan.

"It looks as though it's falling down."

"Gentlemen are not welcome here after ten P.M. Breakfast is at half past eight. Come back then."

"You must have a bunk somewhere," said Farquarson.

"A naval gentleman! Are you the one that made that speech?"

"What speech?"

"The one about sex. Ho, ho, ho," the old witch screamed. "I wish my old man had lived to hear that. Twenty-seven, indeed. That would have shown him."

"Shown him what?" said Farquarson.

"He thought he was a big one, he did. If he'd known the way you admirals go on, he might not have thought so much of himself, isn't that right? Ho, ho, ho."

"Look, I'm not here for laughs, I just want three hours' sleep."

"You? Sleep in bed? Why, according to your speech—"

"It wasn't *my* speech, you disgusting old dandelion," said Farquarson. "I don't know where you read such stuff, you should change your morning paper. Before we both die of old age, just find me a bed."

"They're all full."

"Well, find the one that's least full."

"There's a girl—well, a young woman—well, a woman—alone in Number 54."

Farquarson banged furiously on the ledge of the wooden kiosk where the harridan sheltered.

"A solitary bed, you old bag. Quick. Now. Or I'll wreck the whole crumbling dump, I'll pull down the columns, everything will come down, girls, young women,

women, mature women, old women, women older than the rocks among which they sit—that's you—before you can count three."

He got a bedroom in the end. But it had been like cashing a check at the bank—damned difficult.

It is possible to get by train from Seaford to London, and on Monday morning Farquarson managed it. He bought some newspapers while the train loitered in Lewes station and there it was:

SOHO HIT MAN SLAIN BY BULGAR BROLLY

He was due to fly to Scotland in the afternoon. After a long, tedious, jolting journey, he arrived at Victoria.

When he got to the Highlanders he found that Mr. Camelot did exist after all. Angry letters had begun to appear in an elegant copperplate handwriting. It wasn't surprising. In an age when most fathers had given up worrying about their daughters' casual copulations, a man called Camelot with handwriting like that and origins in Barbados was bound to be the exception. But what difference did it make? A paternity order—a bit later on? Camelot had picked the wrong man for paternity orders; he should have stuck to pointing out Farquarson's mistakes in "arranging the fleet," as he called it—according to Pettina.

Farquarson posted the letters on to the editor of the newspaper that was negotiating for Gwenda's bedroom memoirs. The idea of this was to wreck the market for Gwenda, put the price down, show that just as good—or bad—material was available elsewhere.

At Toothboy's insistence, he and Vraismouth met again the next day, Monday. Whenever Vraismouth set eyes on Toothboy, he felt as though he needed a strong drink, quick, quick. This time he was going to get it, since the meeting took place in the lounge bar of a smart hotel rather than the austere police station of the day before. It was a long drive for both of them, and Vraismouth couldn't see any point in the meeting. He'd been on the telephone half the night. Toothboy carried a daily paper, the one with the headline, "Soho Hit Man Slain By Bulgar Brolly." He pointed at it and said, "That's the key."

They were in comfortable armchairs today, large drinks close to hand on a glass-topped table.

"The key to what?" asked Vraismouth morosely.

"The whole thing. I'll tell you what happened."

"Do you mean to say"—Vraismouth puffed and purpled and bristled—"that you've dragged me all this way as though I were your damned Watson, Hastings, Potson, Pastings? To listen to theories by the hour, by the yard, by the league? I suppose it's Farquarson again. I could invent it all myself if it wasn't obviously such cock."

Sir William Toothboy proceeded relentlessly, gaunt and measured: "Consider the times when Farquarson is known to have been in London, when his presence there can be proved or strongly inferred." And he proceeded to consider them, on and on and on. Toothboy's theory, in effect, added up to a fair simulacrum of what had really happened. But since no one could prove or confirm any of this except Farquarson, it was a matter of academic interest—but to whom? Not to Sir Terence Vraismouth, who listened fish-faced, eyes glazed, bristles drooping, appalled with boredom.

When he could get a word in, he said, "What about the saw? The bough of the tree? The car tracks? The trousers?"

"We have discussed the trousers before. The only important thing about the trousers is that they were much too small to fit Farquarson."

"A *very* important thing."

"Mrs. Broadhill borrowed the saw from a nearby farm. Presumably she cut off the bough. Presumably she meant to return the saw later. The car tracks, goodish prints, are a dreadful waste so far, but you said yesterday that Mrs. Farquarson's car had vanished. And that's the only car we've heard about, apart from the one that got blown up and the old museum Land Rover."

"Someone threw a car off Beachy Head last night," said Vraismouth. "The Chief Constable of Sussex says it's unusual. At least, it's unusual if the car turns out to be empty, as this one did."

Hawkshaw/Toothboy pinned a glittering eye on Vraismouth.

"How do you know it's empty?" he asked.

"They sent down divers at low tide, early this morning. And—this bit should cheer you up—it's Mrs. Farquarson's car."

"Eureka," said Toothboy.

"And what do you eureke from that?"

"The tires, the car tracks."

"It's going to take several weeks to pull this one out of the sea. It's a heavy car. Anyway, they haul them up in batches, apparently. They send barges and heavy lifting gear along when the weather's fine and when they know they'll find a good few cars scattered about the seabed— that's off Beachy Head, of course. Meanwhile they just check to see whether the cars have corpses in them. If they have corpses in, they drag out the corpses. If not, they leave them there for routine salvage."

"Can't they take the tires off?"

"Look," said Vraismouth, "have you ever tried mending a puncture, changing a wheel? It's not too easy on dry land. These divers are clever fellows, but they can't get wheels off from beneath thirty feet of water. Not even to amuse Holmes, Wimsey and Co."

"It's just Farquarson's style," mused Toothboy, "slinging expensive cars off cliffs. More evidence gone bang. Where was Farquarson yesterday afternoon and last night?"

"Obviously there isn't a man following him, since you're the only person in the world who believes all this rot about Farquarson. Then, as usual, he was seen here and there in the course of the day, in London. No one except you thinks of Farquarson as a *murder* suspect, everyone's too busy trying to invite or hire him to make after-dinner speeches. He's worth a thousand pounds a go now, apparently; I don't know what on earth we're supposed to make of that, but there it is.

"Now, I've been listening to all this stuff of yours"— this wasn't true—"and I'll tell you the reality. Just suppose, imagine, conceive—let's go bonkers—that you're *right*. Suppose your rigmarole actually represents real events, things that happened? What's the next step? Well, there isn't one, that's the whole point.

"We're not dealing with any old Glasgow mugger who you can just toss in the slammer in the hope that a bit more evidence turns up later. This is an *admiral,* for God's sake, a national hero, victor of the South China war, the most sought-after after-dinner speaker in England, you name it. *And he hasn't even got a motive,* unless you call Corriehallie a motive, and *that* doesn't account for Mrs. Farquarson or Mrs. Broadhill—the one that interests you most. No one—no one—not the biggest ass on land or sea would consider for one second even *suspecting* Farquarson unless he had a cast-iron motive, cast-iron opportunity. Motive is almost totally absent. Your mighty concoction about what happened on Saturday isn't even circumstantial, there's nothing really there at all. Farquarson was knocked cold in a brawl in his club at 0100 Saturday morning and put to bed by his pals in his other club, the Highlanders. He was seen in Nobb's at 2000 the same evening, dapper as anything, just a bruise on his chin. In the morning no one went into his bedroom at the Highlanders until 1200 because someone had hung the DO NOT DISTURB sign on the door, and they're quite accustomed to treating hangovers with respect there. They found a note that said 'Gone shopping,' but they didn't find Farquarson. Now I'm told the gossip at Nobb's is that it wasn't shopping at all, it was a woman—so there's another witness waiting in the wings, so to speak. So could he have been at Fort Ethelred? How? It's obvious nonsense.

"Look, even if they could get a tire off the car, and even if it fitted your famous car tracks perfectly, the answer would *still* be nix, nix, nix. As for Silver, your key, what's it got to do with anything? With the Laird? Mrs. Farquarson? Mrs. Broadhill? Suppose my fish experts identify Silver from the battle of the fish markets, what does that do to Farquarson? Nix again, my friend. All the witnesses are dead, assuming, that is, that they witnessed anything in the first place."

"I shall persevere," said Toothboy.

"What you do with your time is your business," said Vraismouth, "but I can tell you, flatly and finally, that unless evidence turns up of an order quite different from anything we've got or guessed at so far, there's not the remotest chance of arresting anyone. And as for Farquarson—it's so farfetched as to be ridiculous even if it didn't happen to be impossible."

Once again they parted with mild acrimony, having disposed of most of the morning but not much else.

In such time as they could spare from totting up their own fees, a gaggle of legal luminaries had decided something. Perhaps "decided" is putting it rather strongly. It was more like a "unanimous recommendation to the trustees"—without prejudice, of course, or, indeed, any real conviction except as regards the aforesaid fees. The upshot was as follows:

Harriet, Emily, and Julie each had large trust settlements of their own, as indeed did Emily's daughter, Victoria. Harriet's money joined Emily's, and this huge sum became united in a new trust of which the income was to be rolled up until certain things happened. The key point would be the birth of a male heir. Should Julie marry and bear a son, the whole fortune went into trust for that son, the mother to have the use of the income and other benefits within the discretion of the trustees during the whole of her lifetime. On her death the full amount went to the son absolutely.

But in about six years' time, Julie would be too old to bear children, so the emphasis switched to Victoria. Should *she* marry and bear a son, exactly the same thing happened as in the case of Julie. But in this event, Julie's fortune was added to the whole on Julie's death, the only course by which the old boy's fortune, now vastly increased by investment and accumulated interest, could become one again.

It would only be when Victoria grew too old for childbearing without having produced a son in wedlock that the wily hand of old Morrison reached out from the grave to

109

twitch this vast accumulation of wealth out of his descendants' reach. At this point the Harriet/Emily funds went direct to certain specified charities, carrying the accumulated interest along with them. When Julie died, her money would go the same way, if she had never borne a son. And the very same thing would happen to Victoria's trust capital should *she,* in due course, die without having borne a son in wedlock.

But at present Julie was thirty-nine. More to the point, Victoria was only eighteen—twenty-seven childbearing years in front of her and up to eighty years of life to come.

The trick, in this family, was to marry and produce a male heir. Also, to avoid being murdered.

Faced with such a wide choice of funerals on the same day, Farquarson could see that in cold reality he was stuck with Colin's. It had nothing to do with personal choice, he couldn't afford to be remotely associated with Harriet, Emily, or Silver.

The gathered pieces of Colin Farquarson, late Laird of Corriehallie, were buried in the yard of a small kirk near his estates, to the accompaniment of eulogies that broke even the elastic bounds of falsehood and hypocrisy that are traditional on these occasions.

After the funerals of her mother and her aunt, the very young, very nubile, and (probably) very, very rich Miss Victoria Broadhill carried her mourning back to Deauville. She was a blonde like her mother, unlike her aunts.

A few weeks later, as the sunlight began to dwindle and fall after another glorious day of passing summer, she strolled along the beach, wandered by the wavelets that lapped softly, without menace. At her side, strolling pace for pace, was the old seadog, Farquarson himself, come to comfort her in her loss—more or less.

Now, as the sunset silhouetted them against the briny deep, Farquarson said, "I'll tell you something interesting. John Wilkes said . . ."

TAILPIECE

"Afterward"—as they say in novels—Farquarson said, "Will you marry me?"

Victoria laughed for minutes, long minutes, a genuine, sustained contralto.

"You didn't think I fell for all that rubbish about some Wilkes person I'd never heard of, did you?"

"Some of us might think so. Well, here we are, aren't we? Good old Wilkes, that's what I say. And what about your education?"

"It was curiosity. I've never slept with anyone so *old*."

"Oh yes?" said Farquarson. "Your curiosity is satisfied, I hope."

"It was more like research into the working parts of ancient mariners."

"Was it? Well, it worked like Stephenson's Rocket, didn't it? Catch a tiger by the tail, and all that."

"I've never heard of Stephenson's Rocket and I don't want to. I can't imagine what it could be. Now I've finished my research, I'm going to get dressed."

"You've never heard of John Wilkes or Stephenson's Rocket, right? What *do* they teach you at school these days?"

"I'm not at school, you know that perfectly well."

"Never mind, it was very jolly. We might try it again sometime—quite often would suit me."

"But not me," said Victoria. "Research concluded, back to people who haven't got one foot in the grave."

She proved to be a genuine termagant, both in bed and out, more than Farquarson had bargained for altogether. Kind, gentle, soft, nubile, rich Miss Victoria Broadhill! Such romantic ideas had been misplaced.

As she was dressing, Farquarson said, "What do you do all the time in Deauville?"

"I resist approaches from decrepit and lecherous persons. I go to discos and parties with the healthy, the young, the beautiful, the *jeunesse dorée.*"

"Fornication and drugs, I suppose. How come you know any French? A lively day in the classroom?"

"They all speak English in Deauville. Most of them *are* English, or American. Hadn't you better put some clothes on and clear off? I heard you had a new appointment."

"That's right," said Farquarson.

He had, too.

Their Lordships of the Admiralty had acted, they had sought sweet revenge, and they had found it. They were fed up with Farquarson, most of all with his winning the war. It was unforgivable. And now he'd become Vice Admiral Sir Peter Farquarson, KCB, DSC, RN; they hadn't been able to stop that either. They couldn't give any *reasons,* of course, for his curious new appointment; everyone had to draw his own conclusions. And the conclusions he was meant to draw were as follows: Their Lordships viewed with Olympian displeasure his disobedience in not flying home, his speeches exalting sex, brawls in West End clubs, articles about seductions in Sunday newspapers, and so on. They didn't know anything about the murders— even Toothboy hadn't dared to suggest this to anyone other

116

than Vraismouth—but various bits of gossip had reached them about the Humbert Humbert transactions, even apart from Gwenda and a few previous sexual scandals in Farquarson's past. In general, the Navy tended to tolerate and even encourage high spirits—it was the stuff eccentric old admirals were made of. But Farquarson was beyond a joke—far, far beyond it.

They appointed him Commander in Chief of St. Kilda.

The Admiralty had acquired St. Kilda under the pretense that it would become a vital strategic base from which to control the western approaches and their convoys in the event of war. What they really wanted it for was to dump Farquarson. It was a truly dreadful place, full of "puffins, fulmar petrels, guillemots, razor-birds, Manx shearwaters, and solan geese." It was all cliffs, except for one tiny harbor, and practically inaccessible for eight months of the year, except by helicopter.

Portakabins, tents, oil tanks, radar and radio transmitters and receivers, a whole mass of gear had been installed at short notice while the weather window lasted. All this was to give some credence to the Admiralty's absurd story about defense of convoys, and the equally absurd impression that there was going to be something for Farquarson to do.

The important point was that they couldn't refuse Farquarson a helicopter. They'd have liked to—that really would have kept him quiet for a time, eight months of the year, with luck—but it just couldn't be done.

Once Farquarson had installed himself in the best Portakabin and given his small naval staff an idea of the kind of regime they might look forward to—prophecies of doom—he began to consider more personal needs. Looking back over a very wide experience, he remembered Pettina. She was good fun, a nice girl, unlike—very unlike—bloody Victoria Broadhill. Why not try it? She probably wouldn't come, but there was nothing to lose.

But she did come. She was bored with the bank. She was bored with her father (dead right, there). She'd enjoyed her dinner at the Savoy, her night with Farquarson. It had been much less boring than the things that usually happened to her. The age gap didn't affect her, she just thought Farquarson was a fine fellow, a fine figure of a man, a great man, an admiral, a rich man, a girl's dream. She didn't, after all, know anything about him except his bank balance and his manners at the Savoy and in bed.

When she turned up among the guillemots, Farquarson had her announced as "Lady Farquarson" and insisted that all his staff called her "milady" or "your ladyship." The idea of this was to annoy Their Lordships of the Admiralty, it was meant to be a stinging little shot in the guerrilla warfare between them. But Pettina rather enjoyed it. The naval staff just had to lump it—anyway, they couldn't be *absolutely* certain that she wasn't Lady Farquarson.

Farquarson didn't suppose that "Lady Farquarson" would last long on St. Kilda. A week or two of sexual delights and she would start hankering for the bright lights, beautiful young men, discos (St. Kilda was short on discos), and so on. But this wasn't what happened. To everyone's astonishment, including her own, Pettina discovered that she was a country girl at heart, or perhaps a blasted heath girl would be nearer the mark, considering St. Kilda. She wandered day after day through blizzards along the clifftops, doting on the razor-birds and Manx shearwaters. She became a lover of birds and solitude, which, it turned out, was all she needed on top of nights of bliss with Farquarson. So everyone was wrong about that, including Mr. Camelot.

Mr. Camelot was wrong about everything. He was determined to take up residence on St. Kilda, though in what capacity wasn't clear. Her ladyship's father, presumably, it was a bit late to act as chaperone, though there might be the chance of some blackmail.

But blackmail wasn't Camelot's idea. What he sought was grandeur, and what could be grander than Farquarson, knight, victorious admiral, famous after-dinner speaker, Laird of Corriehallie? He rang Farquarson from the nearest mainland harbor, the first time they had spoken. Previous communication had been one-sided in that Camelot had written lots of long letters and Farquarson had simply thrown them away.

To add to his other irritating qualities, such as his handwriting, his name, his naval pretensions, and his solicitude (probably faked) for his daughter, Camelot had a high, squeaky voice. He must have been a schoolmaster, thought Farquarson angrily (there wasn't much logic in this deduction, but as it happened, Camelot *had* been a schoolmaster). Farquarson thought the whole thing was absurd, if not obscene; he was ridiculously late for the chaperone bit, it must be money he was after, in which case he had come to the wrong place.

Farquarson told his secretaries to say that he was absent, ill, in conference, abroad, dead; but he knew he'd have to speak to Camelot in the end.

"Sir, I come to visit."

"Not so," said Farquarson. "The Ministry of Defense won't allow it."

"I have a permit. The Ministry say if my daughter allowed there, me also."

"I won't allow it either."

"I come anyway, sir. I buy Portakabin."

"Bought-a-cabin, Portakabin," said Farquarson crossly. He could see, given the whole context of the situation, that he was going to get the worst of this. "How are you going to get it up the cliffs? You won't be allowed in the harbor."

"I hire drifter, sir. I load Portakabin on board."

"You've still got to get it up the cliffs."

"You got yours up the cliffs, I get mine."

"They came from the harbor. One or two were hoisted up the cliffs—we used naval tackle."

"I hire tackle of my own. No problem."

"I'll sink your drifter," said Farquarson, exasperated. "I'll send submarines and strike aircraft."

"No, sir. I come to visit my daughter. I bring my own Portakabin, that's fine."

Farquarson couldn't see a way to stop him from coming. With a bit of luck the non-naval tackle would snap and drop the Portakabin on Camelot's head, but Farquarson didn't like to leave matters to chance. Perhaps . . . no, it wouldn't do.

So the Portakabin failed to drop on Camelot's head. He was soon installed and began to make a frightful nuisance of himself. He spent all day writing letters to Farquarson, which were carried the four hundred yards between the two Portakabins by marines who had nothing else to do. Acres of copperplate, the gist being whether Pettina was being accorded a style to which she was totally unaccustomed. Farquarson used them to light the fire, they were worth even less than pound notes.

The Times periodically penetrated the January blizzards, and Farquarson read the following item with the deepest fascination:

> An engagement is announced between the Hon. Anthony Wistleton-Twistleton of South Parkers, Glos, and Miss Julie Morrison, daughter of the late Mr. James Morrison, of Hampstead.

So that was it.

Farquarson had lost interest in the Morrison cash. He had murdered four people in his efforts to lay hands on it, and he had been cheated. Cheated by Julie. She could have all the Wistleton-Twistletons she wanted. With a bit of luck everything would go wrong, including the failure to produce a male heir.

120

He made frequent trips by helicopter—at Admiralty expense—to Corriehallie. Sometimes he took "Lady Farquarson" with him, which raised a few eyebrows in Grampian society. To replace the old house—God forbid—or build the new one he wanted would cost about £10 million, apparently. But there had at least been some insurance on the old one, and the insurance company actually paid up to the tune of £100,000 pounds. Most of this was owed in debts and mortgages, apart from a bunch of Mafia thugs from Soho who turned up with IOUs and threatened to break Farquarson's legs. But threatening Farquarson had never been a profitable exercise, and he threw one of them into the Findspey.

Meanwhile the banks of the river were cleared, lets arranged, gillies hired, the estate began to make the first tottering steps from ruin toward recovery. But what was needed was money, *real* money. Farquarson didn't *visualize* genteel poverty, careful husbandry, penny-pinching. Most people would regard an admiral's pay and pension as solvency of a kind, but to Farquarson it was peanuts, loose cash.

Pettina took to Corriehallie, but to her it lacked the wild magic of St. Kilda, which just shows what a very extreme sort of girl she was beneath her delightful, pert, redheaded exterior.

Come May, the ferry service from the mainland to the tiny harbor became fairly regular, so also did *The Times,* only one day old now. He sat in his Portakabin, the blizzard soughing around the new-built structure, and opened the paper.

Someone had chopped Julie up with an axe.

Even *The Times* headlines lacked space for the Hon. Mrs. Wistleton-Twistleton, but they were doing their best. He read with the deepest attention, then sent a marine to seize the tabloids that belonged to the sailors.

MAD AXE-MAN SLAYS HEIRESS
BUTCHERY OF LAST TRAGIC SISTER
BLOOD BATH IN CEMETERY.

It seemed that Julie had gone alone in the afternoon to visit the cemetery by the little church near Hastings where both her sisters were buried. Someone had found her there, the tombs, graves, and landscape drenched in blood.

So that was what came of cheating simple seafaring men and marrying people called Wistleton-Twistleton. You got chopped up with an axe. It was a moral story, all right. Justice *seen* to be done—seen by Farquarson anyway, if by no one else. He rolled about in his chair, roaring with laughter and delight, something so rare that Pettina asked him what was up.

"Splendid joke about old Spengler," he said.

Which reminded him of the lawyers and the Morrison trusts. More gaggles of luminaries, more guineas. But by now the situation was really quite clear.

So who'd killed Julie?

Well, there were two thoughts. First, cui bono? No question now, Victoria was the only legatee if she could just get herself pregnant in wedlock and produce an heir. The second thought was Lizzie Borden. People would say an axe wasn't a woman's weapon, but history showed that they weren't always right. For Farquarson's money, Victoria would be pretty useful with an axe, not squeamish either.

He wondered what Victoria's alibi was going to look like. Could she have used a "speed" alibi, such as he himself had done? It would be a coincidence, but deaths in the Morrison family were now so common that the odds against coincidence were less than usual.

So it needed thinking about. He thought and thought. There were possibilities—and anyway, he was curious. He mustn't act too hastily, nor must he let the trail grow cold. Give it a week?

Then he would liven up his helicopter crew; they were getting slack.

This time Sir Terence Vraismouth and Sir William Toothboy met by accident. They had both been invited to fish on one of the great Scottish east coast rivers, none of your rotten old Findspeys, this was a *real* river. In May, too. Neither knew the other was fishing there, and their accidental meeting took place at the fishing hut adjoining two beats. The hut stood beside a huge pool, a famous pool, a great glide of spring water. Vraismouth had had no luck, but Toothboy—needless to say—had caught something, a twelve-pound springer.

"That's a kelt," said Vraismouth. "You should have put it back."

A kelt is a stale, spawned fish, inedible, the angler is obliged to return it to the river.

It wasn't a kelt, of course; Vraismouth knew it, Toothboy knew it, any fool could have told. But Vraismouth could barely tolerate Toothboy at the best of times, and these were not the best of times, since Toothboy had caught a fish and he hadn't. Toothboy would be more than ever unbearable. Luckily, there was some Scotch in the hut—quick, quick.

"That's a fine springer," said Toothboy. "Any fool can see it's not a kelt."

"Any fool needs a drink," said Vraismouth. "Quick."

As the Scotch mellowed them, communication—or at any rate conversation—became a possibility. Both were interested in the murder of Julie, but only as spectators, since strictly it was none of their business. Each had—so to speak—presided over the separate deaths of Julie's two sisters; a common bond of curiosity existed.

They sat in their heavy fishing gear on the hard benches inside the hut, munching pork pies and drinking Scotch, Toothboy long and gaunt, Vraismouth puffing, purple, and bristling. Salmon jumped occasionally in the great pool. Small flocks of oystercatchers dipped and sparkled across the surface.

"Just try and make out it was Farquarson *this* time," said Vraismouth. "He was commanding his troops in St. Kilda all day, everyone saw him there." He chewed his pork pie.

"I must agree," said Toothboy pompously. "But I'm interested all the same."

"What's interesting you this time?"

"The girl—Victoria."

"But she was part of the mammoth binge in Deauville. All those young layabouts, trollops, drunks, drug addicts, and so on, were busy with a forty-eight-hour orgy. They're quite proud of it, apparently, even quite proud of their hangovers, though I'm told they're beginning to feel a bit better by now. They're claiming it was the party of a lifetime, and perhaps from their point of view it was."

"But, but, but," said Toothboy.

"But dammit, the cemetery's in Sussex, near Hastings."

"Yes, but people travel these days, Bangkok one minute, St. Kilda the next. People travel rather fast from London to the Quallar and back, if it comes to that."

"Tell me your latest—well, no, don't tell me."

"She could have flown there."

"On, come, come," said Vraismouth. "And anyway, why an axe?"

"She'd never heard of Lizzie Borden, that was the trouble. She thought only men did axe murders—that comes from seeing too much films and telly. She's a very ignorant girl, apparently."

"How do you know all this?"

"Intuition. Instinct. Induction."

Toothboy was having trouble with his pork pie, Vraismouth noted. False teeth, perhaps? He hoped so, they certainly gleamed a bit for Toothboy's age. He said, "Eyes right, so to speak. But how could she have got there?"

"I guess it was a helicopter."

"*Guessing?*" said Vraismouth. "How are the mighty fallen."

"It would only be about an hour from Deauville. The whole thing could be done inside three hours, including murdering her aunt. Remember, she took a siesta. At least the witnesses thought she did, but as they were all stoned blue, anything could have happened. But from what we hear, the siesta was about two hours before evensong, British time. So there was a perfectly good chance the church and the cemetery would be empty. In any case, she only needed to find one of them empty, with her aunt inside it, to get busy."

"What about all the blood and mess?"

"She didn't know about Lizzie Borden, but she did know about Julia Wallace. She took off her clothes, such as they were. Then she washed herself in the font. It's enough to turn you up."

"It's enough to send you mad," said Vraismouth, "and it seems to have done just that. Who piloted the helicopter?"

"How should I know? I expect he's had problems by now, problems with axes, for instance."

"It's all a load of rubbish. It ought to be Wistleton-Twistleton, I don't believe it."

"Why should Wistleton-Twistleton kill his wife, who was pregnant, as you know?"

"Look," said Vraismouth. "None of this makes sense, it's like all your damned theories. What do you expect our chaps—the police—to do?"

"I expect them to persevere in their duty."

"Do you? Well, I'll tell you what's *actually* happening—or not happening. You sit on your miserable mountain concocting theories, but I use the telephone, I ring up, I speak to people. So just listen."

Toothboy nodded, solemn, gaunt, eager. He was having trouble with his third pork pie.

"Now, the French police say the murder happened in Sussex—at least there's no argument about *that*. So they say it's nothing to do with them, they haven't got a murder and they don't want one. Now our pals down south, *they* say that even if the French police should have a sudden attack of zeal, what's the good? With the damned orgy going on, they can't see how any alibi can exist or not exist—it's a perfect and absolute blank, that's what they think.

"So they'd like another murderer—someone who isn't Victoria. But they haven't got one. This person with the mad name, her husband, Wistleton-Twistleton, he was *weeding the rhubarb*—yes, that's right, I'll say it again—*weeding the rhubarb* in his manor, that's to say in South Parkers, Glos. Me, I didn't think people *did* weed rhubarb, I didn't even think anyone ate the stuff these days. I thought rhubarb was a sort of sex joke, music-hall style. But no, you can't win in this case, and nor can our pals down south. That's what Wistleton-Twistleton was doing and his gardeners saw him doing it. I expect they thought he'd gone mad, but then that's what employees always think about their employers. Anyway, he *must* be mad— Wistleton-Twistleton, South Parkers, rhubarb, I ask you. But he didn't kill his wife, that's the point. And there aren't any other candidates, not one."

"If there had been a helicopter . . ." said Toothboy, and he went on for about a year telling Vraismouth about helicopters.

Vraismouth *knew* there had been a helicopter, at least, some people in the village nearby had heard one. But then they were always hearing helicopters, which were used for crop-spraying, coast-guard duties, taking unsolicited photographs of local villas on the off-chance that the owners could be conned into buying enlargements, flying around on council duties to see if people had secretly built sun patios that they weren't paying rates on, and sundry other rural pursuits; you'd have thought the skies were filled with helicopters from dawn to dusk, at any rate around the cemetery near Hastings.

But he wasn't going to tell Toothboy this, he'd heard more than enough about helicopters already. He wanted to get back to the river now and catch some salmon, one, two, three, it didn't matter so long as he finished the day with more salmon than Toothboy.

Like the Admiralty, the helicopter crew on St. Kilda were also fed up with Farquarson, his capriciousness, and occasional rages. Mostly the blizzards that blew continuously across St. Kilda precluded any flying—the crew were safe in the bar while Farquarson read his *Times* and burned Camelot's letters and played games with Pettina. When flying wasn't obviously suicidal, Farquarson insisted on outings, ostensibly—and indeed usually—to Corriehallie. But he was forever surveying rivers from his seat in the plane, and would suddenly order: "Put me down here."

Then he went off with a rod and often came back with a salmon or two, presumably poached. Meanwhile the crew just twiddled their thumbs, thankful to be out of St. Kilda but otherwise not happy.

But there was much worse to come.

A week after the item in the paper—the murder of Julie—that had given Farquarson such huge pleasure, he told the helicopter pilot that he was going to fly to Deauville.

"It's not allowed," said the pilot.

"We're not in the Brownies now," said Farquarson. "Just fly me there."

"It's impossible."

"Don't be absurd, man. What can they do? They can't shoot us down."

"They just might."

"Fill the thing up and get ready to fly to Deauville."

"We don't carry enough fuel."

"We'll stop at naval air stations and top up. We don't want to pay for the stuff."

"I wish, sir, to protest formally."

"You can protest as much as you like. Meanwhile get me to Deauville."

And so on.

At Deauville, Farquarson didn't venture outside the airport, but they were there for six hours. He had been masquerading as a senior British police officer, a convincing performance because he looked like one anyway. And his papers—Commander in Chief of St. Kilda—were enough to confuse the English, let alone foreigners. They took him at face value. When he rejoined his impatient crew, longing now for the home comforts of St. Kilda, he said, "Next stop Algiers. Off we go."

Short of outright mutiny, the pilot could only make more protests, and so he did. He demanded to have these orders in writing. Farquarson scribbled a note on the back of a sheet from one of Camelot's screeds that he had in his pocket. If anyone ever came to read it, they'd be more interested in the flip side than in the orders to the pilot.

So they flew across France and this time Farquarson *did* have to pay for the petrol. He wondered whether he could think of a way to charge it up.

Then they crossed the Mediterranean.

And then Farquarson disappeared for twenty-four hours into the stews of Algiers.

He was mighty pleased with himself when he reappeared, still looking quite dapper.

"Right," he said. "St. Kilda."

On St. Kilda life pursued its normal, tranquil course, the only consolation being Pettina. The summer blizzards were different from the winter blizzards, but not much; everything else went on as usual.

During a foray to Nobb's a few weeks after his research in Algiers, Farquarson heard a fascinating rumor from Trevor Spengler. Some spy in Deauville had told Spengler that Victoria was pregnant, and as a trustee that had interested Spengler considerably. But so far as the trustees knew, she hadn't married anyone, and showed no signs of doing so. So what happened next?

Farquarson decided what was going to happen next; it was time to act. At last he held all the trumps. At last he'd had a bit of luck. It was true that he could—and did—attribute most of his present advantage to his own enterprise and industry, but there'd been some luck too.

On the trip to Deauville he wasn't going to use his helicopter, he didn't need it. Anyway, there was a fearful row going on about the Mediterranean flight, the air-traffic-control authorities of three countries were up in arms. Their Lordships of the Admiralty, willing to wound yet still afraid to strike, had adopted a very high and mighty tone about the helicopter's flight to Algiers and back. "Misuse of naval equipment . . . misuse of naval personnel . . . reckless disregard for the safety of international flight routes . . . diplomatic incidents . . ." et cetera. More bumf. It joined the latest packets from Camelot in the fireplace or the wastepaper basket.

Incredibly there was no blizzard blowing on the July morning when he boarded the ferry to the mainland in his best tweeds. This time he was going to Deauville the way English gentlemen should, first-class train and boat.

The next day he arrived in Deauville and tracked down Miss Victoria Broadhill easily enough in the bar of the best hotel. It was 1000 hours on a sunny morning. She was drinking something brown in a tall tumbler, kept cool by lots of ice, something that would burn a hole in tarmac by the smell of it. This wouldn't do the unborn child much good—perhaps that was the idea. A very bad idea, in Farquarson's opinion.

Beneath her expensive clothes and momentarily rather dilapidated appearance (a hangover?), she looked like a sexy, rather brawny, blond teenager, which was just what she was. Except for her taste for axes and her evident pregnancy.

"God, not you," she said. "Back from the grave."

Farquarson sat down opposite her.

"Will you marry me?" he said.

"Why not? I'm pregnant, and you can't have long to live."

This was much too good to be true. Perhaps she was drunk.

"Splendid. We'll drink to *us*—but not that stuff, that smells like Fernet Branca and schnapps."

"It's not your child."

"What the hell's that got to do with it? It's the money we're after, isn't it? Who cares where the child came from, it's only got to be male."

"Well, suppose it isn't."

"Then we try again," said Farquarson cheerfully. "Even if we have seven or eight daughters, we ought to get there in the end."

"You really are the most frightful man."

"And you're a frightful girl, right? But how else are you going to get the cash? Why doesn't this fellow—the beautiful youth, the *jeunesse dorée*—marry you? He should

131

be able to put up with you in exchange for so much cash, just as I can."

"He's married."

"That wasn't very clever—but then you're not very clever, are you? Why can't you marry another of the *jeunesse dorée?*"

"They don't want someone else's baby."

"I must say, the youth are getting a bit above themselves these days. Whoever heard such a fuss about the brat having the wrong father."

"I shall do what I like," said Victoria. "And I need someone to marry. I've wondered about my mother's death, that's another thing. And Aunt Harriet's. And the first time you came to Deauville."

"If you're going to say things like that, the sooner we get married the better, to save yourself an action for slander, apart from the other advantages. But then *I've* wondered about Julie's death. In fact, I've done more than wonder. Some women are very handy with an axe—and you're a good strong girl, I know it."

"I couldn't have been there, in Sussex."

"Couldn't you? I've been thinking about that. You see, I *went* to the airport in Deauville, a special trip. And then I went to Algiers. I know about your alibi. I found your pilot."

"I was with friends all day—everyone knows that."

"It was your siesta—that made me wonder."

"You're just a foolish old gentleman. A girl needs a little sleep in the middle of a party that went on nonstop for forty-eight hours."

"Well," said Farquarson cheerfully. "It's all water under the bridge. Why didn't you kill your helicopter pilot? He's a right rogue, I must say, he never would be missed."

"I never got a chance. There wasn't time. I gave him thirty thousand pounds."

"You may be a fiend in human shape," said Farquarson. "But the trouble is, you're not very bright. We shall make a splendid pair as we march up the aisle."

"We're marching to the registry office," said Victoria. "And the sooner the better. I'm fed up with the *jeunesse dorée,* and the great advantage *you* have is that you can't last long, you're too old. Once I've got the money, you'll oblige me by falling off the perch as fast as you can."

"If you're thinking of some future axe-work, or something similar, just remember I'm not a poor unsuspecting woman visiting her sisters' graves in a country churchyard."

"Don't fret," said Victoria. "Anno Domini will do it."

So Vice Admiral Sir Peter Farquarson, KCB, DSC, RN, and Miss Victoria Broadhill made their way to an up-market registry office in London, witnesses dragooned off the street. To the rustle of trust documents they were bound in wedlock, cemented by the threats of exposing each other's murders on the one hand and the enticing prospect, on the other, of wealth beyond the dreams of avarice.

Farquarson had bought Pettina a croft on Mugg. He hadn't actually paid for it, but in half an hour's time he should be able to afford to post off a check.